I0741591

SACRIFICIAL LAMB

©2020 Ashley Nicole

All rights reserved. No part of this publication may be reproduced, distributed, or transmitted in any form or by any means, including photocopying, recording, or other electronic or mechanical methods, without the prior written permission of the publisher, except in the case of brief quotations embodied in critical reviews and certain other noncommercial uses permitted by copyright law. For permission requests, contact the publisher listed below.

Published by
Dark and Twisted Press
P. O. Box 1064
Moorefield, WV 26836

ISBN 978-1-7347191-2-3
Library of Congress Control Number 2020906905

This is a work of fiction. Names, characters, businesses, places, events, locales, and incidents are either the products of the author's imagination or used in a fictitious manner. Any resemblance to actual persons, living or dead, or actual events is purely coincidental.

Cover designed by Ryan Rinsler
Edited by Michele Sagan

First Edition

Visit www.ashleynicolewrites.com to learn more.

SACRIFICIAL LAMB

The Other Angels Book One

By Ashley Nicole

Prologue – Kathryn

His light fingers leave a trail of warmth along my cheek. My eyes meet his blue ones and we begin to lean in. The meaning behind this kiss feels heavy as if this moment has always existed and been waiting here for us, building up intensity in anticipation. The electric between us charges the air into something almost tangible. His breath mixes with mine in the closing gap between our lips.

The vision that encompasses my mind rips away and leaves me standing with my hands in cold dishwater. How long had I been standing here? And why do I keep having these powerful daydreams?

No, not daydreams. They're stronger and more vivid than simply getting lost in thought. They capture my entire being and take me on a trip far away. But where? And with who?

I never see his full face or hear his name. But he knows mine. He's called me Katie in countless dreams, the longing of being with me clear in his voice.

I pull the plug in the sink and dry my hands. The soft carpet in the living room welcomes my bare feet. I draw back the curtain screening the window on my front door. The darkness swallows the houses on my street, and the path into town is empty except for two angels leading a girl toward the forest. Their hands are clamped around her arms and it appears she is struggling to break free of their hold.

But that wouldn't make any sense. Not here anyways.

PART ONE: KATHRYN

CHAPTER ONE

My head is spinning. The black spotted vision of the world around me comes in and out of focus making the nausea harder to ignore. But I must ignore it before he notices I'm not okay. One deep breath. Two. My mind whirls as I grasp for words.

"Today was gorgeous!" Sitting in the grass next to the picnic Scotty put together, I lean back on my hands and close my eyes as the evening sun warms my face.

"Not as gorgeous as you." Scotty stands up and offers me his hand.

"Do you ever get tired of being a cheeseball?" I ask as I take his hand and let him pull me into his embrace, thankful for the stability his arms offer. I inhale his woodsy based cologne.

"Not at all. I'm surprised you still put with me." He pulls away enough to look at my face. I stare into his eyes. Their shade is such a delicate blue resembling ice crystals forming when the sun hits them just right. I trace the shape of his clean-shaven face with my eyes, all the way from his chin to the top of his head where his black hair hangs a little more unruly than usual.

We gather our crumpled chip bags and half empty jars of peanut butter and jelly. I neatly fold the red checked blanket while mentally grounding my dizzy self before returning to Scotty's side. He grabs the picnic basket in one hand and my hand in the other as we walk around the lake that sits in the middle of the seemingly endless green fields of the town park. Ducks glide across the glossy water, their distant honks mixed in with the soft tweets of small robins perched in the trees above my head. When the path narrows, a fluffy white rabbit scampers away from us, disappearing over the hill.

"Have you been okay lately? You seem a little distracted today." Scotty pulls me out of my daydreaming, stopping our stroll and making me look at him.

"What do you mean?" I bite my lip and avert my gaze from his worried expression, hiding behind a curtain of light blonde hair.

"You know what I mean, Katie." He lifts my chin, so I have to look at him. "Is the medicine helping? Are you still feeling overwhelmed and anxious?"

My stomach starts to turn again. "I'm alright, Scotty. No need to make a fuss out of this."

"I'm not. I just care about you and want to make sure you're happy, which is harder to do when we're apart."

I sigh. "I know, but I'm fine. I've been happy today with you, haven't I? It's better when I don't think about it." Most of the time.

"Okay, just know that I love you."

"I love you too."

We start walking again. I know he's worried about me. My family is too, but they shouldn't be. Whatever has put me into this slump will pass and I will be okay again.

Feeling overwhelmed, my heart begins racing again. My mind returns to just two months ago during the semester's move-in weekend. The college prepares a big meal on the quad for students and their families every year. I had my parents and Scotty with me but somehow in the mass chaos of hungry bodies, I'd become separated from them. I remember the sharp jabs of panic in my stomach and the tightness in my chest as I struggled to get enough air into my lungs. It felt like it was never going to end, until it did, with me blacking out. I've grown up with mild social anxiety and don't like being around a lot of people, but it's never felt that intense. The doctors said it was a panic attack and put me on some medication.

I seem to be doing better now. I don't have those attacks anymore if I take the meds, but when I think about it my heart beats a little harder and my mind clouds. I need to work harder to stay in control.

I turn my attention back to the unseasonably warm March day. The fresh air cradles the exposed skin peeking out from my white and yellow sundress. The weather hints at an early return of spring, evident by the horizontal lines that cut across the freshly mowed grass. A pleasant light breeze rustles the rainbow of colored feathers intertwined with my long hair.

"I have one more surprise for you." Scotty again pulls me from my thoughts.

"How can there possibly be more? You've outdone yourself this time." Warmth radiates through my body.

Scotty leads me to the weathered, wooden dock and we sit on its edge. I unstrap my white sandals and dip my toes into the chilly water.

"Close your eyes," he instructs.

I obey and feel the cool metal of a necklace as he hooks it around my neck. My eyes fly open and I look down to see a heart-shaped silver locket with my blue Sapphire and his yellow Topaz birthstones on the outside. I open it to see a black and white picture of Scotty and I from our senior prom and a quote that says, "Love never dies."

"A locket?"

"I know you like classics." His triumphant smile lights up like a fourth of July sky.

"It's perfect. Thank you." I lean in and kiss his lips softly, savoring the warmth of his face so close to mine.

"Happy three-year anniversary sweetheart." He kisses my forehead then I rest against his shoulder and watch the sun sink lower into the glittering lake. My internal storm calms and I welcome the peaceful silence that hangs between us.

As the last traces of light disappear below the horizon, we wander back up the streetlamp lit path. I watch moths flock to the murky yellow lights and hover as if trapped in an invisible fence. I wrap my arms around myself as the dropping temperature brings goosebumps onto my skin. Scotty's truck sits in the parking lot that has emptied with the setting of the sun. The beaten older model white Ford may not look impressive, but Scotty is proud of it. The summer after he got his license, he worked every odd job the neighbors offered to make enough money to buy it himself.

The door squeaks in protest as he opens it for me. My bare legs rub against the ripped fabric as I slide into my seat. I click the seatbelt into place smiling to myself recalling the first time I rode in this truck.

Our first date during our Junior year of high school, we went to the movies and had dinner at the local diner. Scotty drove me home and worked up the courage to kiss me, but as he leaned in his seatbelt locked up leaving his face inches from mine. I giggled and told him his truck must be jealous and left him kiss-less. A little cruel maybe but as soon as he got home, he texted asking when he could see me again.

Now, as he pulls the truck over in front of my house, I turn to face him, a playful smile dancing on my lips. "Is your truck jealous tonight?"

In the dim lighting offered by the dashboard lights, I watch Scotty cringe. "I'm never going to live that down, am I?"

"Not if I have anything to say about it." I slide to the middle seat and unhook his seatbelt. He caresses my cheek with his hand before bringing his lips to mine. I slide even closer and intertwine my fingers into his hair. This whole day has made me realize how much I've missed the closeness of him. We fall into a heavier kiss and the windows start to fog. I break away and sigh. "I've missed you."

"I've missed you too. Try not to stay away so long this time, okay? A month is a long time to make my lips wait for yours."

I feel a sliver of guilt seep in. "I'll try. I'll have to see how my work schedule is. I love you."

"I love you too."

I steal one more kiss before slipping out of the truck. Automatic porchlights flick on and illuminate the stone walkway that leads to the white front door of my small brick home. Once inside, I shut the door and lean against it, sliding down to the light brown hardwood floor. How lucky can one person be?

Anna's old ears finally hear me. Her toenails click on the floor as she races toward me, the wag of her fluffy tail only outdone by her ecstatic barking. Her being fifteen and myself twenty, most of my memorable childhood years include her. The tinges of grey that touch her golden face in no way diminishes the twinkle of affection in her amber eyes. I truly miss her when I'm away.

"Kathryn? Is that you?'

"Yeah, Mom." I kick off my shoes and skip to the kitchen,

giddy as a schoolgirl who got kissed on the bus. Mom stands at the sink doing dishes in the faded yellow kitchen. Her graying blonde hair is swept up in a bun with a few loose strands hanging over her shoulders. She's wearing the sunflower apron I got her this past Christmas. The warm smell of the roast she made for dinner still lingers in the air. I slide in next to her and begin drying the clean cups and plates.

"So, what did you and boy wonder do today?"

"You would think after three years you'd warm up to him. I've never understood why you call him that."

My mother smiles. "It's not an insult if that's what you're asking. I just remember a few short years ago you didn't have much interest in dating and then this young man shows up and sweeps you off your feet. I just think he must be some great guy to love you the way he does."

My nose crinkles with laughter. "He didn't sweep me off my feet!"

"No? Tell me about your day then?"

I take a handful of clean silverware from the dish strainer and begin sorting it in the drawer behind Mom. "He took me on a picnic at the park and we went walking around the lake and sat on the dock to watch the sunset."

Mom clatters some plates into my side of the sink. "That sounds very nice. Most boys just want to take you to their bedroom."

"Scott's not like that. He wants to take care of me not sleep with me." I watch Mom scrub at a spot on a skillet. We've always been close and open about everything, but since she's right about me not being interested in boys prior to Scotty, these kinds of conversations didn't come up much. After a few moments I break the silence. "He thinks you don't like him."

Mom puts the skillet down and looks directly at me with a hand on her hip. "Well, you need to tell that boy he's crazy."

I can't hold back the smile that forces its way onto my face. "I love you, Mom." I throw my arms around her neck and hold her tight. "Thank you."

"Where's my hug?" I turn around and see Dad's broad frame standing in the kitchen doorway. I rush to him and throw my arms around his neck. He squeezes me tight. "I haven't seen you for four weeks, kiddo."

"Sorry, Dad. I came in late last night and you were already asleep in your chair, then Scotty and I were out all day for our third anniversary." I pull away and look at his balding head and the laugh crinkles around his warm brown eyes.

"Your mom told me. How was it?"

"It was great." I walk back over to the sink and finish putting away the dishes. He disappears into the living room. I smile to myself betting he'll be asleep in his recliner by the time I head upstairs to go to bed. He's one of the hardest working men I know. Owning his own construction business, he sometimes words fifteen to sixteen hours a day, weekends too. Although he makes a point to never miss a birthday or any other special occasion, he is gone a lot of the time.

Mom glances at me as if she wants to say something but is unsure if she should. I wait patiently until she speaks. "I ordered a refill for your medicine yesterday. You can stop and pick it up tomorrow on your way back to college."

I stiffen. "I could have done that back in Keyser."

"I know, but I thought you were probably getting low and I know you're busy through the week, so I was trying to help." She fiddles with her dishcloth as she tries to sound nonchalant.

"Thanks." My mood drops as I think about my anxiety governing my life.

"Have you been doing okay on them? You haven't had any of those attacks at college, have you? You know the doctor said if they don't work, we can see about changing to a different kind."

"Mom, they're working fine. I wish everyone would stop asking about it." I try not to sound snappy, so my voice comes out as a forced calm.

"I'm just worried sweetheart. I was really scared that day you passed out from your anxiety." She places a hand on my shoulder, and I feel myself melt. It's not her fault I feel like this.

I sigh. "I know, but I'm alright. Really. I'm going to bed now, okay?"

"Alright, Kathryn. Goodnight. I'll see you in the morning."

"Night." I walk through the living room placing a quick kiss on my sleeping dad's forehead. Anna follows me up the carpeted stairs, passing collages of family pictures on the way to my room. I plug in a strand of lights inside the doorway. The rainbow bulbs wrap around the room and light up the dozens of photographs attached to the pale blue walls with decorative tape. In my small connecting bathroom, I only flip my nightlight on, enjoying the relaxing ambience of the dim lighting. I splash cool water on my face and allow myself to breathe vowing to myself that this anxiety isn't going to control me anymore. After brushing my teeth, I wander back into my bedroom.

I flop down on my bed and rub the silky pink comforter. Anna hoists herself up beside me and lays down. It's been a long day. I start to think about my trip back to Riverside tomorrow and the upcoming Calculus midterm looming in the near future.

I groan and roll over, too tired to change into pajamas. It doesn't take long for me to drift off to sleep.

CHAPTER TWO

"Now Cain offered some of the fruits of the land to the Lord, but his brother Abel offered a burnt sacrifice of one of his sheep. The Lord accepted Abel's offering but rejected Cain's, which made Cain angry and bitter toward his brother." Mrs. Barren strolls around the small young adult Sunday school room with her message Bible spread open in her wrinkled hands.

"I'd be angry too… fresh fruit beats burnt sheep any day." Cassie sits with one foot propped up on her metal chair with her phone in her hand. I occasionally throw questioning glances at her slouched position and lack of interest.

Mrs. Barren glares at her overtop the large round glasses perched at the end of her nose but keeps a calm voice. "Not to the Lord. A blood sacrifice is much more pleasing because of its similarity to the sacrifice of Jesus later. Abel had faith of what God wanted where Cain did not. The Lord warned Cain that jealousy is the threshold to sin, but Cain didn't listen. Instead, he lured his brother out into the field, picked up a rock, and killed him."

I run my fingertips over the flimsy pages of my Bible. The worn black cover is hidden by my bright yellow case. Mom gave it to me when I graduated high school and said it was her mother's. Holding it and reading from it makes me feel connected to Grandma even though she passed away when I was only five. I hope I meet her in Heaven someday.

"Mrs. B, as exciting as this is, it's 12:00 and I'm leaving." Cassie pops out of her seat and bustles out the door. Her mane of bright blue hair flowing behind her.

Mrs. Barren sighs and closes her book. "She's right. The rest of you enjoy your afternoons and we will pick up with our read through in Genesis next week."

I gently close my Bible and slide the zipper around the case. A frail hand comes to rest on my shoulder and I look up to see Mrs. Barren's kind smiling face. "I've missed seeing you in my class, Kathryn. And where is Scott today? Did he not come home from school this weekend?"

"Scotty says he's sorry about missing class this week but he's helping his mom box up some things." I glance at his empty seat beside me. "I've missed being here though. I always learn something new from your read throughs."

"There's always more to learn. Even when you get to my age. Well, I better go collect my grandkids. I hope you have a wonderful week at college." She strolls out the door into the crowded hallway as all the classes begin to empty.

If I even make it to her age.

The dark, invasive thought feels foreign like it's not my own. Regardless, I feel my heartbeat start to quicken. I have to get out of here.

Hastily, I throw my Bible into my backpack and push through the tightly packed hoard of people. Outside my lungs start to work harder. My breaths become quick and forced as my chest tightens.

In the safety of my little blue Toyota sedan I let the sobs

out before they can choke me, wishing Scotty was here to help calm me down. My shaky hands rummage through my purse until they find a small orange prescription bottle. Even though I consistently take my normal dose in the mornings, I've found lately I need a second one most days. I pop the round white pill into my mouth and swallow, noting how low my supply has become. I guess it's a good thing Mom sent a refill in for more.

Leaning back and shutting my eyes for several minutes, I let the medicine take hold. I feel the weight lift, the pressure release, the tension ease. It feels like somebody flipped the panic button back off and everything is okay again. After a few more deep breaths, I'm steady enough to drive the short ten minutes home. Maybe it's a psychological thing that I feel better so quickly after taking the extra dose. It's like someone up above is rewarding the bad behavior of overdosing. Or someone down below. Is this what dependence or addiction feels like?

When I pull into the driveway, Mom walks out of the house with an envelope in her hand. She's still dressed in her pale pink blouse and white pants. Her adult church class must have let out a little early this week. She slips the letter into our mailbox then walks with me into the house.

"Did you want to go have lunch at the diner before heading back to school?" She tucks a loose strand of hair behind my ear.

"Actually, I think I'm going to leave as soon as I change into something more comfortable." I glance down at my light blue button up and tan dress pants.

"You're trying to skip out early?" Her brows knit together.

My cheeks flush. "I have a big test to study for." It's not a complete lie but I still feel a little rush of guilt. I don't make trips home on weekends often since I normally work, but the longer I'm here the higher chance of her seeing me have a weakness in sanity.

"I guess that's a valid excuse." Her face softens. "I'll tell your dad you said you love him."

"I can call him tonight." I bound up the stairs and replace my stiff clothes with black sweatpants and a plain purple T-shirt. Anna watches me from my bed. I scratch behind her ears and kiss the air in front of her nose. "I'll be back old girl." Her tail swishes against the bed covers.

Back downstairs, Mom follows me outside. "Now are you sure you have everything?"

"Yes, Mom," I say as I shove my suitcase in my trunk and walk around to the driver's door where she's waiting expectantly.

"You better call me when you get there."

"You know this isn't the first time I've ever driven to college. I will. No worries." I give her a big squeeze and slide into the driver's seat. I roll down the window and turn the catchy pop music up.

"Don't forget to stop and pick up your medicine," Mom yells at the last minute as I start to drive away. I give her a thumbs up out the window.

Once out of our neighborhood and on the highway, I reach for my phone and click Cassie's name in my contacts. I roll my windows up and the rings come through my car speakers until she picks up. "Hello?"

"Hey, what are you up to?" I hear her click off the music playing in the background.

"Just chilling in my room. You?"

"I'm headed back to Riverside, but I wanted to call and ask what was up with you in class today?" There are some muffled sounds as if she's squirming uncomfortably. I let the silence stretch on as I watch the distant Appalachian Mountains fly by my windows.

"I don't know why I acted like that," Cassie's small voice finally answers.

"You know, you choose to be there, no one makes you, so I know you want to learn. You shouldn't act disrespectful. Church is a safe place."

"You're right. I guess I let some stress from home carry over today. I'll be more attentive next week."

"I know what it's like to have other things going on inside, but don't let them ruin the good stuff going on too." I bite my lip, feeling a little hypocritical.

"Okay, I'll work on it. Thanks for calling, Katie. It does mean a lot knowing someone cares."

"Anytime. Call me if you ever just need to talk, and call Mrs. Barren to apologize," I add sternly.

"I will. Catch you later."

"Take care." My thumb hits the end call button on my steering wheel and the upbeat music fills the air once again. Don't let the bad ruin the good. I can do that.

And Cassie can too. She moved in with the Miller's, a few houses down the street from mine during my senior year. Judy and Roy had two other foster kids that were going to college and I think they were dreading an empty home. Cassie had just started freshman year and was a bit of a troublemaker from what Mom had told me. Mrs. Barren asked me to befriend her to help her settle down.

As far as forced relationships go, this one went unexpectantly well. Cassie warmed up to me and even let me talk her into trying a few church lessons. She said she always looked up to her big brother and having me around felt comfortable and familiar. I was a rock for her.

Now, when I'm away at college, she starts acting up again. I think part of her is afraid she's going to lose me like she lost her brother. Early on in foster care, he was adopted when she wasn't, and she hasn't been able to find him. I need to remember to call her more often to keep her grounded.

A small, humorless laugh escapes my lips. How is it that I can keep someone else grounded when I have no say over my own chaotic feelings? I need to take control.

Two hours later, I find an empty parking spot to pull into behind my dorm building. The large three-story structure casts shade over the parking lot as a few other cars pull in, all of them returning from their short weekend away. I grab my purse from the passenger seat and unload my suitcase from the trunk.

It's nice to be back. I love home but I feel so independent and free here.

I ride the clunky elevator up to the top floor. When I unlock my dorm room door, I hear a shout from the far side of the room. "Welcome home roomie!"

I prop my suitcase up on my desk chair and walk over to Marie's bed to give her a hug. She lays down the book she was reading and wraps her arms around me.

I couldn't have asked for a better roommate. Marie and I became instant friends when we were paired as roommates as freshmen last year. Her optimistic, bubbly, outgoing personality never has trouble making me smile. She is a few inches shorter than me with hazel eyes that pair perfectly with her red tinted brown hair that hangs down to her waist.

Thank goodness we get along because our dorm room is fairly small. Sliding door closets line one side of our short hall and the bathroom, the other side. In our main room, our bulky beds with built in drawers sit at opposite corners while our desks are pushed up against opposing walls. We each have our own decorative style, making it clear whose side is which. While mine reflects my colorful bedroom at home, Marie's is adorned in darker, rustic colors.

"How was your weekend?" I ask absentmindedly as I send a quick text to Scotty and my mom, letting them know I've arrived safely. I begin to unpack my now clean clothes from my suitcase.

"What are you doing asking me about my weekend? I sat around here studying and you and I both know your weekend is what we should be talking about!" She watches me with genuine interest.

I laugh lightly. "There's not too much to tell. Scotty and I just went on an incredible date and he gave me this." I hold out my locket away from my neck.

Marie crawls out of bed and rushes over. "It's beautiful!"

I blush. "It is, isn't it?" I allow myself to trail off in my thoughts. I'm so lucky to have found Scotty. Or rather, to have been found by Scotty. It's hard being away from him for so long but we're both in college, working hard to create a stable life for ourselves, for our future. I had never focused as hard on my studies as I have after meeting him.

That reminds me.

"Oh! I have a Calculus test to study for! I have to do better on this one! Sorry, Marie, I'll be back to talk later!" I snatch my Calculus book up off my desk and rush out the door.

One of my favorite places on campus is on the quad, right in the middle at the flagpole. I love to be outside to study, listen to music, or just people watch. I find it more relaxing than staying cooped up in my room or fighting for a comfy chair in the too quiet library.

I sit on the short brick wall surrounding the flagpole and prop my book open. In my notebook I begin to work through the sample problems. If I stay focused, I will understand this. Guitar strums drift across the breeze and lull me into a comfortable rhythm of problem solving. My ears tune out shouts and conversations so well that I almost don't respond to someone speaking to me.

"Is this seat taken?"

Startled, I look up from my notes to a broad tan body shrouded in sunlight. I squint trying to make out a face, but what little I can see doesn't look familiar.

"Umm… no." I awkwardly slide sideways on the rough brick seating. I catch a glimpse around me and see that no one else is sitting on the wall. Why does he have to sit right next to me?

I try to steal a glance once he's sat down out of the sun but he's full on staring at me. Instead of looking away, I can't help but to stare back. The stubble on his chin leads up his prominent jawline. His light brown hair lays in a I-just-got-out-of-bed style. Most striking are his green eyes that shine like dew kissed grass.

"I'm sorry for staring but you look so familiar. What's your name?"

I continue to stare. Make words! I look away. "Uh, sorry, I'm Katie." I allow myself another peek but this time his eyes look silver like the reflective blade of a knife. Must be the sunlight messing with my eyes.

"I thought that was you. You don't recognize me, do you?" He slides closer and I fight the urge to slide backwards.

"Should I?" Something pulls at my memory, but I can't quite grasp it.

"I'm Matthew. We went to middle school together." He waits expectantly for recognition to kick in.

After a brief moment, my heart skips and my breath catches. Matthew and I had been so close when we were younger. He was my best friend. I couldn't believe that this guy sitting beside me was really him. When I knew him, he was an awkward disproportional thirteen-year-old. Now…now one could call him hot. Or I could.

My eyes slip to his left arm. A gold bangle hangs loosely

around his wrist. I scan his forearm for a long, faded scar that's barely visible but I know where to look. I recall the day he bet me I couldn't beat him on my bike down a rough trail at the park. Exposed tree roots and rocks made a speed run dangerous, but I wasn't about to back down from a challenge. Even though he was winning the whole way, he kept glancing back to make sure I was okay. That caused him not to notice the rock his front tire hit. I let him wrap his arm up in my favorite pink Lion King jacket to stop the blood and we walked back to his house where his mom doctored him up and made us cookies.

Returning to the present, I look at him in awe. "I don't know what to say… I can't believe it!"

"How about you say yes to my next question?" Matthew flashes me a flawless smile and my heart jumps at how amazing he looks.

I stare at him without replying for a moment too long. My head stops swimming and I blink a few times before stammering, "W-what question would that be?"

"Let me take you out to dinner." The way he phrases it isn't at all like a question, but rather an opportunity I'd be crazy to pass up.

"You mean, like a date?" I blink a few times, stunned at his forwardness.

"If that's what you want to call it." His smile turns into a teasing one which only makes my heart pound harder.

"Okay, I mean… no. I mean, I can't." I trip over my words trying to get them straight, "I have a boyfriend."

"Ah… I should have known as pretty as you are you wouldn't be single." His smooth voice makes my cheeks warm. "How about we go out to dinner and not call it a date?"

"I don't know…" I try to think reasonably but with his silvery eyes looking me over it's hard to concentrate.

His shoulders slump and his lower lip pokes out ever so

slightly. "Aw, Katie, come on. It'll be fun. We can catch up on lost years." He looks up at me with heavily lashed eyes.

No part of me wants to say no. So, I don't. "Okay, Mattie."

CHAPTER THREE

"Would you like to come back to my room? You can meet my roommate. She's the greatest." I gather up my books and look at Matthew. He does look really good. It's too bad he moved away; we could have had something.

What am I thinking? I have Scotty. Matthew is just my friend from the past. My brain doesn't seem to be thinking clearly.

"Sure. That sounds perfect." We start walking across the lawn back to my room. He places his hand on my lower back. I know I should pull away, but I don't. It's like the little voice in the back of my mind, the sane one, has taken a vacation.

"So, where have you been?"

"Originally North Carolina, but then some things happened, and I was on my own for a while. I found some new friends who showed me the world a little differently and that helped."

"How so?" I find myself hanging on to every word, almost as if he was hypnotizing me. His smooth voice caresses my ears.

"I'll let you know soon." He drops the conversation and I'm left to puzzle over the reason why.

My steps quicken as we walk through the crowded main floor of my dorm building where hungry students stand in lines for food. Matthew's gaze floats across a few faces like he's looking for someone but keeps up with my hurried steps.

Back at my room I unlock my door and step in. Matthew follows and looks around. "Well you sure decorated the hell out of the walls." He smirks at some of the Bible verses I printed out and taped up, but I pretend not to notice. Not everyone is religious, and I try to respect that.

Instead I blush. My dorm walls echo the ones back home as every blank space is occupied by photos, printed out quotes, and strings of colored lights. "I'm sorry, I like to be creative." For a moment an awkward silence hangs over us until I break it by addressing the obvious. "I guess Marie went to get food. I'm not sure when she will be back."

Matthew turns his attention from studying one of my family photos back to me. "Well, isn't that lucky? I'm sure we can find something to do to pass the time until she gets here." His husky voice is suggestive, and I begin to feel a little uneasy.

"I told you, I have a boyfriend." I watch him wearily and rub my palms against the sides of my pants.

"I know, Katie Cat. I'm not going to do anything you wouldn't want me to." He flops onto my bed and gestures for me to join him. "I'm only saying we can talk while we wait."

My heart begins to beat even harder than before. I will my voice to sound strong. "Don't call me that, please." I sit on the edge of the bed. Why do I feel like this?

His deep green eyes drill into me and then with one blink they turn silver.

How does he do that?

Suddenly I don't feel as nervous. The fear drains out of

my body. What am I worried about? He's my friend. He's not going to hurt me. I lay on my side to face him. He doesn't try to grab me or pull me in like my earlier fears led me to believe would happen. Instead, he lifts his hand to gently stroke my cheek. "I wish I could have found you sooner."

Sooner? Before I had a boyfriend? Or before something else?

I place my hand over his. I fight the urge to bring it to my lips to kiss. Just friends. But I want more. All I have to do is surrender…

I feel myself leaning in…

And then the door clicks open. I bolt up into a sitting position out of Matthew's reach, stunned. What am I doing?

Marie closes the door. "Katie? You here? I have something crazy to tell you -" Her voice cuts off when she looks up and sees Matthew. "I'm sorry, am I interrupting something?" She looks at me tilting her head to one side.

"No, no. Marie this is an old friend of mine, Matthew. We haven't seen each other in years. I brought him up to show him the room and meet you." I blush knowing my exaggerated hand gestures probably look silly.

Luckily, Marie doesn't seem to notice. "Oh, hi, Matthew. Nice to meet you." Marie extends her right hand and Matthew stands to complete the handshake.

"Likewise." His face is smiling but I watch his eyes drill into Marie. I sense that the two are sizing each other up, both wary of the other.

After a few more seconds, but what feels like hours, Marie begins to shift from one foot to the other. "Well, it's nice to meet you, but can I talk to Katie alone?"

Matthew raises his eyebrows. "Hope I'm not stepping on anyone's toes." He walks to the door. "See you around, Katie." The door clicks behind him and I turn to stare at Marie.

"What was all that about?"

"I really don't know. It felt like he was looking at me, but more than you are right now. It was weird. I just don't feel right about him." She walks to her side of the room and lays her keys on her messy desk, piled with loose papers and stacks of fantasy books.

"But you don't even know him." I start putting away the clothes that I had hastily left out earlier.

"Yeah, that's the weird thing, I'm really not one to judge strangers but I instantly got a bad vibe from him. The air in this room was thick when I came in so unless you guys were having a heated argument or making out, there is something off about him."

I flush at the memory of almost kissing Matthew. That was strange. Why would I let myself get that close? Scotty would be crushed.

Scotty…

Guilt grabs ahold of me and squeezes tight. How could I almost do that to him? My breathing goes shallow and I feel lightheaded.

Marie places her hand on my shoulder. "Katie, are you okay? You look like you're going to puke or pass out. Did you take your meds today?"

Her face is filled with concern. My mouth is dry, so I just nod in answer to her questions. She herds me into the bathroom and lets me slouch to the floor while she turns on the cold water. She soaks a washcloth and kneels beside me to pat my face with it. My pulse slows and my head clears a little. "Thank you, Marie," I croak.

"No problem. I'm just glad I could be here. You scare me lately." She smiles down at me.

"Can I have a moment alone?" Marie purses her lips but agrees. She walks out and shuts the door. I curl in on myself.

I feel so overwhelmed inside. I almost cheated on Scotty.

What is wrong with me? My breathing picks up again and my hands become shaky. Sweat beads on my forehead as my thoughts swim like they're in a tsunami. I press my nails into the palms of my hands, gritting my teeth at the slight pain.

No.

Don't let the bad ruin the good. Take control.

I relax my hands. I'm okay. I reunited with my best friend and nothing happened that would ruin what Scotty and I have. I don't need to get worked up like this. Nothing. Happened.

I get back to my feet and emerge from the bathroom. Marie sits at her desk and looks up from her book. "You good?"

I feel a hint of embarrassment for having Marie take care of me in my moment of panic. "Yeah, thanks. I'm sorry about that."

"No problem. I get it. It's what friends are for." She closes her book and lightly taps it with her thumb as she gauges whether she should ask her next question or not. "Did he do or say something to you to get you worked up?"

My eyes grow wide. "What? No! We were friends in grade school. He moved away the summer after sixth grade."

Marie's shoulders relax. "Okay, I just wanted to check. I'm glad you found your friend again, but he still seems off to me. Just be careful." We let the conversation drop. She rummages through the drawers under her bed for pajamas then slips past me toward the bathroom. Moments later I hear the shower water running.

I glance at my phone. Almost 7:00. Dad should be home, so I give him a quick call.

"Hey, kiddo." His voice is heavy with exhaustion.

"Hey, how was your day?" I slouch in my desk chair and doodle absentmindedly on a piece of scrap paper.

"Not too bad. Long, but aren't they all? I missed you this morning. Get back to Keyser safe?" Dad sounds tired but he's still Dad.

"Yeah, I drove back right after church so I could do some studying. I just wanted to say I'm sorry I didn't get to spend much time with you while I was home." I scribble out the frowny face I drew.

"That's alright, honey. I know you had plans with Scott. He's a good boy. How about next time you're home you and I can plan a date? We'll go to the diner and play putt-putt or something."

"That sounds great! Spring break is in three weeks, so I'll have plenty of time to spend with both of you."

"Good. Well, I better go help your mother with dinner. I'll talk to you again soon. I love you."

"I love you too." I put down my phone and open my vet tech book. Just because I need to study Calculus more doesn't mean I shouldn't study my other subjects. Plus, I like this one best, so it's a nice change of pace from studying Calculus earlier. I read through the chapter and make flashcards of the section questions. Marie reenters the room and begins doing some studying of her own. Time slips away from me.

My phone begins to buzz, and the screen alights with Scott's picture. It startles me at first but then I answer. "Hey, Scotty."

"Hey, Katie. What are you up to?"

I glance at Marie who waves her hand ensuring me that I'm not bothering her. She's playing on her phone instead of doing homework now anyways. "Just studying. You?" I go and lounge on my bed against a mound of pillows.

"Packing my clothes."

"Packing? You haven't left for Pennshire yet?" I glance at the darkened sky outside the window.

"I'm not going back until in the morning. I've been helping Mom pack more of Dad's stuff away this weekend. And since I spent Saturday with you, I didn't finish it all."

"Oh, I'm sorry." Scotty's Dad decided to leave him and his mom about a month ago for a younger woman. I know it's been hard on them both. I secretly think Joyce believes he's going to come back since she won't get rid of his things. Scotty has only recently convinced her to pack it away, hoping by not seeing it will help her cope and move on.

"Katie, you have no reason to apologize."

But I do. I think about telling him about Matthew. Holding my new friend as a secret doesn't feel right but telling Scotty about a new guy in my life right after talking about his cheating father doesn't feel right either. It's not the right time now. Guilt seeps in turning my inside cold. "I just know it's hard," is all I can manage to say.

"It'll be okay. Mom and I are tough. Mom has me, and I have you."

"Right. Well, I'm going to go shower and get ready for bed. I'll text you before I go to sleep, okay?"

"Alright, Katie. I love you."

"I love you too." I lay down my phone and take a deep breath, letting it out slowly. I'm okay. I'll tell him tomorrow.

I grab my pajamas from the end of the bed and shuffle to the bathroom. The heat from the shower steams up the small space as I slowly undress. Tomorrow is another day. Another chance for things to be better.

CHAPTER FOUR

My Monday morning classes pass without much excitement. Scotty sends me an early text ensuring me he made it to Pennshire safely. I use the grab and go option for lunch and meet up with Marie outside by the flagpole. We chat about how unfair it is for teachers to have pop quizzes and laugh as two jocks try to catch the same football and collide with each other.

Matthew strolls by, only pausing long enough to touch my shoulder and tell me I look pretty today. Marie watches him but doesn't say anything. I shout in my head for him to come back, but I'm glad he can't hear me. It's best to keep him at arm's length until I can sort through yesterday's strange emotions.

After lunch, I drop off my books in my room and grab my car keys. Even with my scattered thoughts and overwhelming feelings I can't help but feel excited to return to work after the weekend off.

JoJo's Jungle is an exotic pet store with animals ranging from cats to snakes to prairie dogs. I started working there at the beginning of last semester and can't imagine being happier anywhere else. Joe, the owner, a short round man with a grey beard and sparkling eyes only works me a few hours a day to cooperate with my class and study schedules.

I park my car in the tiny gravel parking lot and lock it. On days I don't work until close, I enjoy the short walk through town from campus to work, but it's not one I would do at night in a college town. I open the door to the little shop nestled between an insurance office and an abandoned building. The bells hanging on the inside handle harmonize with the twooting birds in their cages hanging from the high ceiling. No one is sitting at the register desk, so I slowly circle the room to make up for being early.

The left wall has shelves of tanks holding different kinds of snakes wrapped around branches and lizards chilling in water bowls. We have one snake, a green reticulated python, that's seventeen feet long. Dwayne takes him out to hold for fun, but I've only worked up the courage to stroke his scaly skin. Working here definitely expands my comfort zone but I enjoy it.

Tucked in the corner is the turtle pond. The constant flowing fountain adds a peaceful vibe to the shop. Next to it is the fish tanks on the back wall. All the bright swirls of colors make the tanks look like liquid rainbows.

A sharp yap pulls my attention to the right wall where the dog and cat kennels are. A young golden retriever wags its tail so hard its whole butt wiggles. I stick my hand in between the bars and laugh as she excitedly licks my fingers. Her bright amber eyes remind me so much of Anna's. I often wonder which weekend trip will be the last time I see her.

"There's our pet whisperer." Dwayne strolls out from the back room where we keep our animal food and other supplies over to where I'm daydreaming. His shaggy blonde hair hangs in his blue eyes. "Can you change the bedding in the rabbit pens and feed the fish?" He pushes his glasses up on the bridge of his nose.

"Of course." Thoughts of home fade away as I easily flow into my work routine.

"We have a new type of fish there on the bottom. They eat the tropical pellets."

"Got it." My knowledge of animals grows with each day. That's what I enjoy most about working with exotics. More potential to learn something cool.

Cleaning pens and feeding animals is about all I'm asked to do but I don't mind. It allows me time to handle all the pets, and that makes me happy. Occasionally I have to help a costumer or work the cash register but usually the guys handle that since they know the prices and the market better. They've been working for Joe since he opened the shop over ten years ago.

I go to the back room and grab the basket we keep our assortment of fish food in. Who knew different fish actually preferred differed food? I begin adding pinches of smelly flakes to the tanks when suddenly I'm showered with sprinkles of cold water. I jerk my head around to find Leo standing beside me laughing. His dark mischievous eyes hide in the shadow of his long black hair and his tan hand glistens with water.

"Whoops! You looked a bit gloomy, so I thought I'd be your rain cloud." He dips his fingers in the turtle pond and flicks them at me again.

My lips twist into a sly smile. "It's not just calling for scattered showers. There's a storm coming." I cup my hand in one of the fish tanks and fling the water into Leo's scruffy face. Dwayne walks out of the back room and laughs at Leo's dripping hair.

All three of us break out into a fit of laughter. This right here is why this place is my favorite place to be. I'm not going to continue letting my emotions be stronger than myself. The dinging of the bells on the door makes us all look up. Joe saunters in assessing what is in front of him.

"Are you guys making a mess again?" He looks at the wet spots on the scuffed grey tiles.

"Would you believe some rain clouds busted in here?" Leo asks still grinning broadly.

"I'll get a mop and clean it up." I head to the back room unable to hide my own smile.

"Now see? Katie is a proper employee unlike you two boneheads. I don't know what I'm going to do without her." One corner of Joe's mouth lifts but the smile doesn't reach his eyes.

Without me? He must mean when I graduate. That's not for two more years though so he shouldn't be down about that. I shake the thought and mop up the water.

The see-through rabbit pens sit in the middle of the room with open tops so that customers can reach in and pet the critters' soft fur. I put the mop away and grab one of the large bags of fresh sweet-smelling wood shavings. The strong pine scent fills my nostrils and masks the other scents of the store temporarily. I drift on the aroma into an easy routine of evening cleaning.

A few hours later I look up at the clock as my shift is winding to its end. "Joe, I'm headed out. Do you want me to come in right after class or wait for the closing shift tomorrow?"

"Leo won't be in after four so you can fill his place until closing." He runs the sales receipt from the register and taps out numbers on a calculator. Reading glasses perch at the end of his nose and his eyebrows scrunch in concentration.

"Okay, I'll see you then." I open the door and breathe in the chilly air.

"Thanks for your help," Joe calls and waves without looking up.

He's so kind. I always feel so light inside after work. I feel like I'm important and that I really make a difference, and I love playing with the animals.

Outside, the evening sun is beginning to dip behind the trees and casts an orange light that reflects off the street's shop windows. I unlock my car and open the door. As I'm about to shut it, someone reaches out to stop me. I look up into the deepest green eyes only inches from mine. They remind me of an evergreen forest swept up in a wildfire as they glow in the sunset.

Matthew is bent over leaning in my door. "Hey, Katie Cat. How was work?"

I swivel in my seat so that I am facing him. "How did you know I worked here?"

"Oh, I talked to Marie. She's not that bad once she warms up to you."

"She really is sweet, but why would she tell you where I worked? Not that I mind since it's you, but considering her initial opinion of you, it just seems strange of her to hand out that information."

Matthew waves a dismissive hand. "We had a good talk. She understands we're friends now. I'm much more interested in your opinion of me."

"My opinion of you?" I avert my eyes but then feel embarrassed for not answering so I look back to meet his gaze and find myself staring into his silver eyes. "I think you have beautiful eyes." The words tumble out of my mouth before I can catch them. I start to feel fluttery inside like the feathers from the birds in their cages in the pet shop.

"Can my beautiful eyes convince you to give me a ride

back to campus?" He bats his long brown eyelashes in a playful manner.

"Sure." No part of me wants him to leave yet. He slides into the passenger seat and I start the car. "Why were you here anyway?" I ask casually.

"I was out for a walk and decide I wanted to see you." He flips through my CD case which was laying on the floor at his feet.

My heart speeds up. Really? I bite my lower lip. The thought of him being interested in me excites me more than it should.

He flashes a CD at me. "You still listen to Linkin Park?"

"Only that album. It was our soundtrack, remember?"

"How could I forget? We used to scream those lyrics like we were real badasses." He erupts with laughter and my earlier apprehensions lift. We would bring his radio to the park and sing those songs at the top of our lungs. Jumping over tress and across rocks, we put on the best concert.

In no time at all I pull my car into the dimly lit parking lot. Matthew gets out and walks around to my side. Once out of the car, I catch myself staring again. I don't know where these strong feelings are coming from, but I can't deny I'm attracted to him.

"I'd invite you up to the room again, but I don't want to jinx Marie warming up to you."

My phone buzzes in my pocket. I glance at the screen to see a notification signaling a text from Scotty saying, "Hey, Katie, what's up?"

"I agree." Matthew tucks a finger under my chin to make me look back at him. His touch causes my entire body to tingle. "I definitely want to see more of you and that would be hard if she keeps kicking me out."

The way he says he wants to see more of me makes my breath catch. He must have heard it because he leans in without hesitation and locks his lips onto mine.

I don't resist. I can't. Every part of my brain is screaming that I want this. We press up against my car and his kiss becomes more persistent and hungrier. I finally break it and gasp for breath. He winks at me, smiling broadly, and turns his back to walk away.

My phone buzzes again with another text from Scotty, "I just want you to know I miss you." Followed by several hearts.

I can't find the words to reply. I just stand there, tingling, craving more.

CHAPTER FIVE

What have I done?

Walking through the back door of my dorm building I start thinking clearly again.

I kissed Matthew. Why? What was I thinking? I wasn't thinking. All my emotions became so strong all at once. That seems to be happening a lot lately.

What do I tell Scotty? I can't tell him. Can I?

My head is spinning too fast for me to keep up. Maybe if I ask Marie, she can help me make sense of this.

No, I can't tell her either. What would she think of me then?

Guilt threatens to drown me and I feel physically sick. I push open the restroom door on the main floor and run into the first of three stalls. I hang my head over the toilet grateful no one else is in here because all that comes out is heavy sobs.

I sit back and lean against the door. I feel the coolness of the dingy yellow tile through the butt of my blue jeans. My chest begins to hurt with the pounding of my heartbeat. Is it echoing? Or is that just in my own ears?

Take control. I need to distract myself. I glance at my phone, the screen is black, then quickly push it across the floor. No way will that help. I shove my hands into my pants' pockets. My right hand emerges with a crumbled gum wrapper and a bit of wood shavings from work. In my left hand the sleek metal of my pocketknife comes into view.

The reflective metallic rainbow distorts my face. Scotty bought the knife for me last year when I first came to college as a means of protection for myself. I've never had to use it for more than opening packages but maybe I need to use it now. I flick the blade out, prodding my pointer finger with the sharp tip. Other than digging my nails into my palms, I've never thought of hurting myself before, nor have I fully understood why others do it, but right now I feel enlightened. I apply more pressure.

A single drop of blood runs down the length of my finger onto my hand. I pull the knife away and watch the red trail darken with another drop. Realization hits me as I notice my heart rate has slowed. My head clears and I take a few more deep breaths.

My legs are a bit shaky as I stand but I don't feel overwhelmed anymore. I wash what's left of my smeared makeup off my face along with the blood on my hand in the sink and start walking to my room again.

I unlock the door and cautiously walk in. I have to act normal. The room is mostly dark other than the glow of the computer Marie is looking at on her desk and a string of my rainbow lights she must have plugged in for me. Marie looks up from her laptop. "Hey girl, you okay? You look pale."

Uh-oh. "Yeah, I'm good. Just tired. It's been a long day."

"I hear you." She stands, grabbing her pajamas, and heads for the bathroom to shower.

A part of me doesn't want to be alone. My finger prick has clotted but the immediate pain from when I accidentally

36

tap it against something is still there to remind me. But the small elation that I stopped the overwhelming feelings helps. I am in control.

I decide to call Mom. I know I need to talk to Scotty, but I can't. Not yet. I only wait a few rings in before she picks up. "Hello?"

"Hey, Mom. It's me." I flop onto my bed and crowd myself with pillows. Seeking closeness and comfort.

"Hey, Kathryn. How are you doing today?" The soft murmurs of the TV plays in the background.

"I'm good, I just got off work and I wanted to ask you something."

"Sure, what is it?"

"Do you remember my friend Matthew from middle school? The one who came over all the time until he moved away?" I'm not sure why, but I hold my breath until she responds.

"The one who passed away about a year ago?"

My body freezes. "No, that can't be the same person. Who are you talking about?"

"Are you sure? I remember his mother called one day to let us know since the two of you were close. I think she said he got mixed up in a wrong crowd and was into drugs or something."

"I think you have him confused with someone else."

"Maybe you're right. Anyway, what about him?" The pause stretches on for several seconds. "Kathryn?"

"Nothing really. I was thinking about him today for some reason and wondered if you remembered him. That's all."

"Of course, I do. He came over almost every evening and he had the brightest green eyes I think I've ever seen."

"You remember his eyes being green? Not a silver or silver green?" What color did I remember? Why is it so hard for me to know for sure?

"Definitely green. I'm sure I have some old photos of you guys in a book around here somewhere. I can pull them out for you next time you're home if you want?"

"No, that's okay. Anyways, I have to go. I have a little bit of homework and Scotty should be calling soon."

"Are you sure? You sound a little upset? Did you take your medicine today?"

"Yes, I'm fine, just wanted to chit chat for a little."

"Alright, well I love you."

"I love you too." I press the end button. Who would have called Mom? I didn't have too many friends growing up. It obviously wasn't Matthew's mom though. Marie saw and talked to Mattie so it's not like I'm seeing ghosts. Right?

I crawl out of bed and change into some blue fuzzy pajama pants and a black Riverside College t-shirt. I begin to brush my hair out when Marie emerges from the bathroom, her wrapped up in a towel. She glances at the clock on her phone. "I know Scotty will be calling soon, but I have an English paper to finish tonight…"

Her voice trails off, but she doesn't have to ask. I smile, taking the hint, happy to help my friend. "I guess I can go roam the halls for a little while," I tease. The more time that passes from when I kissed Matthew the lighter the weight bearing down on me feels. Him kissing me was a misunderstanding, which we'll discuss next time I see him. It doesn't change anything from here on out.

Marie gives me a big appreciative smile as I slide out the door. I start pacing the full length of the hallway outside our room. I've memorized the hotel style pattern of the carpet from the nightly talks I've had here with Scotty. The green, blue, and yellow loops overlap on the brown background. My pink fuzzy slippers make no noise as I pass by the other dorm rooms. Some are quiet with students probably studying and others erupt with sounds of music, movies, and other, more active activities.

Right on the 8:00 dot my phone buzzes and alights with Scotty's picture. I hesitate for a moment willing my voice to sound normal as I answer. "Hey, Scotty."

"Hey, sweetheart. How are you?" His soft voice caresses my fading guilty conscience.

"I'm good. You?"

"Not bad, a bit tired since I drove to school before classes and work, but I'll manage. Just means I'll sleep good. Did you go in to work today?"

"Yeah, it was fun. The guys and I got into a water fight." I want to smile at the memory, but I need to tell him about Matthew. Keeping him a secret probably allowed for tonight's kiss to happen. This needs to be out in the open. Why is this so hard? It's okay that I have a new friend, even if we are close.

"It's really starting to bother me that only guys work there with you." Scotty's tone and voice grow drastically cold.

I blink a few times momentarily caught off guard by his sudden change. I think I've only heard him angry a handful of times since we've been together, but never once at me. "Are you okay? You sound really upset all of a sudden." Does he already know about Matthew?

"Oh, I don't know, maybe I'm jealous of all the time you spend with those guys." His voice is heavy with sarcasm.

"Scott, it's my job. I work with them, that's it. You've never said anything about this before?" I feel tears sting my eyes and I push open the door to the nearest stairwell which usually offers privacy thanks to the well-used elevators.

"Sure, Katie." The silence hangs thick between us.

What do I do? I feel like I'm having to defend myself when I'm completely innocent and he doesn't believe me. But I'm not completely innocent, am I? The guilt starts to crawl back in. My stomach turns. I think about coming clean and telling him what happened with Matthew, but as I think of this uncharacteristic anger growing, I back out. I reach into my mind for a different subject. "How is your sculpture project coming along?"

"Great, actually." And just like that a switch is flipped and his voice softens. "I have a great idea that will tie you and I into the theme."

"Really? How?" I breathe a sigh of relief that his brief anger spell has passed. Maybe something at school happened and I hit the trigger reminding him.

"You'll have to wait and see." I hear the playful note in his tone. I can't help but smile until his voice brings me back. "So, what do you have to do this week? Didn't you say you had a big test coming up."

I cringe. "Yes, I have my Calculus midterm tomorrow."

"How do you feel about it?"

"Nervous. I did awful on the last test and I can't afford to do that again."

"You'll do great, Katie. You're so smart."

"Thanks. I hope you're right." We sit in a comfortable silence for a few seconds until I yawn. "I should probably get to bed. I'd like to go over my notes one more time in the morning."

"Alright, Katie. Goodnight. I love you."

"I love you too. Night." I hang up and walk back to the room. I don't know what I'd do without him. His confidence in me has settled my rattled nerves. Whatever happened today with Matthew will not happen again and I will make that very clear to him.

Marie is still typing away when I enter our room. In the bathroom, I brush my teeth and cleanse my face. As I look into the mirror, I take some deep breaths. Everything is going to be okay. I have studied hard for this test.

I crawl into bed and pull the covers up tight seeking comfort. I drift off to sleep dreaming of Scotty's anger and my mistake.

CHAPTER SIX

I wake up feeling terrible. I silence the wailing beeps from my alarm clock that fuel the headache that's been brewing all night from the overthinking and lack of sleep. My sticky eyes open to the dark room. Predawn light seeps through the curtained window. I still feel guilty about what happened with Matthew. I know I won't let it happen again but how could I have done that to Scotty? Could Marie be right about him being bad? And I'm absolutely dreading the Calculus test I have coming up in only two short hours.

I trudge to the bathroom sink and run cold water to splash my face. I need to wake up so I can try studying a little more. I get dressed as quietly as I can while keeping an eye on Marie's sleeping form.

I open the medicine cabinet above the sink. I don't know why I've started feeling like this. I swallow an anti-anxiety pill wondering if they're even working. Managing my anxiety has never been a problem. I know to avoid certain situations and remember to breathe. Why is it becoming harder to do that now? Lately everything has me upset and no matter what I do

I can't shake this feeling of dread.

I don't understand what is sending me into this downward spiral. It's true I just created a problem in my relationship with Scotty that I need to work through, and my grades need to be a little better, but in the grand scheme of things I'm doing okay. I made it to college, I have a wonderful family, a caring boyfriend, good friends, and a job that makes me happy. What is so wrong that it has my emotions jumping off a cliff? Is there something wrong with me?

I stare at the bottle in my hand. They're not working. I've been on them for two months and I feel no different, unless different is meant to mean worse. But I know I have to stay on them. It makes those around me feel better. I don't want anyone worrying about me, and I especially don't want them knowing about the new knife thing I used to supplement the medicine.

As I put the bottle back, I catch my reflection in the mirror. Wisps of blonde hair hang in my face and curl around my eyes. Eyes that look empty and dull today. My thin, fair-skinned body lacks the curves to be noticeably attractive but that's never stopped my love for dresses before. Today it's hiding under yoga pants and a hoodie.

It's another warm day, and while I know other college girls will be taking advantage of the comfortable temperature by wearing shorts and tank tops, I pull my long sleeves down over my hands and grab my backpack to head out the door.

I'm one of the first few students to enter the dining hall. Smells of greasy sausage and carb loaded pancakes almost entice me to fill a plate but instead I grab a bowl of cereal. I slip into a booth tucked in the corner away from the chatty tables dotting the middle.

Swirling my spoon around the soggy lumps, I flip page after page through my notes. Some of it actually makes sense to me as I follow the steps. I just need to memorize the methods of the ones I don't understand.

I check my watch and bolt out of my seat. With only ten minutes left, I fly across the quad. I can't be late. I need the full class period to take the test.

Halfway across the field, I notice a girl from my vet tech class being pushed by a much larger guy. His loud voice carries across on the wind to me as he calls her harsh names. She holds her books up and tries to shrink behind her dark hair. The guy brings down his right hand and slaps her load out of her arms, sending papers scattering across the ground. "Stop trying to hide from me, freak!"

I can't take it anymore. Before he can reach for her again, I push myself between them and stare at the bigger male. "Back off!"

His hand becomes motionless in the air as he looks me over, sizing me up. "Get out of my way. This ain't your business."

"This is my classmate, my friend, that makes it my business. Don't try me." Although I've never interacted with the girl outside of class the guy seems to believe me. Rather than having two witnesses against one, he lowers his hand.

"Whatever, neither of you losers are worth my time." He stalks off, being sure to steps on several loose papers on his way.

I bend down and help the girl gather her things. She looks at me through her thick round glasses. "You didn't have to do that."

"Of course, I did. I couldn't let him treat you like that." I hand her the stack of her things.

"Well, thank you. Not many others would have done that. I'll see you in class." She hustles off to her destination as I realize how late I'm becoming for mine.

Standing at the door to the classroom building I am rushing to is Matthew. He smiles and puts his hand on the door handle. "What was that about, Savior Katie?"

As I draw closer, I try to be quick. "I can't talk right now. I have a huge test that I'm running to." I reach for the handle since he doesn't open the door, but he grabs my hand.

"Who said anything about talking?" He encircles his fingers around my wrist and pulls me closer. Our chests touch and he kisses me deeply. I instantly get lost in the heavy kiss. I'm sure some people are staring but I don't care. I feel so alive. It's like all my life force that was missing this morning is right here. My test anxieties begin to melt.

He releases me and without a word, turns his back and walks away. My eyes follow him, wishing he hadn't stopped. He calls over his right shoulder, "Don't fail your test."

Right then I feel like I have been slapped in the face. Don't fail? Was that supposed to be a good luck? I walk into the building with a sick stomach. I'm more unsure about the test now than I thought I was.

An hour and a half later the professor reluctantly takes up my test, at least fifteen minutes after everyone else had left. I walk heavily out into the hall and slump against the wall. I really don't know how that test went.

I cross my arms on my knees and put my head down feeling defeated. In just moments, I feel a presence in front of me. I lift my head expecting to see a concerned professor, but instead it's those green eyes.

I don't know how, but ever since we reunited, he always seems to be around when I'm drowning in emotions, "How do you do it, Mattie?"

"How do I do what?" He squats down to my level.

"How do you always know where to find me?"

He gives me a smug look, like he knows something I

don't. "Let's just say I have a feel for your emotions."

Was that supposed to sound sweet? My brows scrunch together in puzzlement. He's like a giant riddle sometimes. Well, all the time.

He offers me his hand and I allow him to pull me to my feet as he stands. "Are you finished with classes?" he asks as he snakes his arm around my waist and guides me down the hall. I should move his arm, but my thoughts are starting to steady and I can't help but to think it has something to do with him. Maybe it's the familiarity. But Scotty wouldn't be okay with this. I should distance myself a little more. But it feels nice to be comforted.

"I am for a few hours. I think I'm going to go back to the room to de-stress. Would you like to join me? I could make us some tea." Maybe asking him to hang out isn't smart, but I want to keep our friendship. Then I can tell Scotty that he honestly is a friend. So, inviting Matthew to my room is a step in this. And I could use a friend now anyway.

"I don't know about the tea, but I can definitely help you de-stress."

I look up into his silver eyes and shiver with pleasure. I don't know what he has planned but I want to find out.

"Ahem." I squirm out of Matthew's hold and turn around finding myself staring at Marie. She has her hands on her hips and a glare that is drilling holes into Matthew. "How was your test, Katie?"

I blush. This isn't going to be a fun conversation later. "I'm not sure. I guessed a lot but I'm hoping with all the work I showed I will get enough partial credit to save me."

"Hopefully." Her voice is flat and laced with disapproval.

"Yeah, well I'm going to go back to the room to make some tea. See you later." I scramble to get out of there.

We make a quick stop to the Student Union where our mailboxes are. In mine is a slip of paper informing me I have a package, so I pick it up from the office. "Do you want to check your mail while we're here?" I ask Matthew as I check the label on my box. It's addressed to me from Scotty.

"Nah, there wouldn't be anything for me." He waves dismissively and follows me out of the building.

"So, why doesn't Marie like me?" Matthew asks as I unlock my door.

"She just doesn't know you yet and she has a bad first impression of you. I have a boyfriend and you and I have been acting so close." I bite my lip. Matthew and I need to talk.

In my room, Matthew lounges on my bed while I start heating some water in my electric kettle. I open my package from Scotty. Inside is a pack of Skittles and a Dr Pepper along with a not that says, "I hope this finds you when you need it most. Remember that I love you and am so proud of who you are".

My heart swells with love. Right here, right now, I choose Scotty and I will always choose him.

"Mattie, you can't kiss me anymore." I try not to look at him, knowing those stupid silver eyes will make me lose focus. They are silver, aren't they?

"Why's that?"

"Because it's not right." I can't continue kissing him and lying to Scotty. Isn't it obvious to him like it is me?

Matthew appears disinterested in my argument as he flips through the planner I had left on my bed. "What's not right about it? I like it and you like it, so no harm done."

This time I do look at him. I know there was a reason he shouldn't kiss me, but his words are so believable. I forget why I even mentioned it.

My water clicks off and reminds me that I was making tea. I pull out two red mugs and put a tea bag in each. I pour in the hot water and add four spoonfuls of sugar to each mug. Matthew watches me with his nose crinkled. "That's an awful lot of sugar."

My shoulders turn in and I feel a heat creep across my face. "I'm sorry, it's a habit. Let it sit and the tea will get strong enough to dull the sweetness."

"I think you should let yours sit too." Matthew's eyes track my every move.

"Why do you say that?"

He props himself up on his elbow and holds out his other hand. "Come here."

I obey without question, laying down beside him so that I can stare into his green eyes. His gold bangle hands around his arm that's propping his head up. "This is pretty. You been wearing it every time I see you. Where did you get it?" I trace the shiny metal with my fingertips.

"The friends I mentioned before, the ones I said helped me see the world differently, they gave it to me. Without it, I wouldn't be able to see you and those beautiful eyes of yours." He brushes a few loose strands of hair from my face.

"Mattie…" I start to protest even though a part of me wants to let him continue.

He gently takes my hand. "You don't want me to kiss you, so I won't. Let's talk about the good old days of middle school instead."

We get lost in reminiscing as our two mugs of tea grow stronger and colder.

CHAPTER SEVEN

"Katie, we need to talk." Marie lays down her book as I look up from my Biology notes.

"About what?" I try to play dumb, but I know where this is going.

"You know damn well what I'm talking about." Marie sounds angry, but her concern breaks through.

"I know." I look away. I feel like a small kid about to be lectured. The past week and a half have gone by patterned by my talks with Matthew and my phone calls with Scotty. Although there hasn't been anything romantic between Mattie and I, he still laces our frequent conversations with light touches to my hair or cheeks. Scotty hasn't had any more anger outbursts either and I've grown comfortable with how things are. Maybe too comfortable, but both guys take my anxieties away and I don't want to lose that.

"You've been spending a lot of time with Matthew in the past few days, and from what I've seen, it's as more than friends." She narrows her eyes at me.

I lower my chin. "I know sometimes it seems bad, but

things have changed. We sat down and had a talk about it all and we're just friends now. Like how it used to be."

Marie watches my face. I know she wants to get her point across, but she also knows how fragile I have been and doesn't want to upset me too much. "How does Scott feel about your new friend?"

"He doesn't know about him yet." The heavy guilt that associates itself with the thought of Matthew and Scotty weighs on me.

"This isn't like you, Katie. You can't keep this from him. It's not right and it's not fair to him. You have to tell him about Matthew or if you can't then admit there's more going on and break it off with Scott. You can't have both."

"I know." I can't bring my eyes to meet hers.

"And personally, I hope you choose Scott. He's so kind to you. I don't like Matthew. I think he's taking advantage of you."

"You don't understand, Marie. I don't know what it is, but I'm so compelled by Matthew when he's around. I forget all about my anxiety and problems and I'm swept up in the strongest desire I have ever felt. I surrender to him without knowing I'm surrendering, but he knows I only want a friendship, so nothing more has happened between us." Other than the two previous kisses, but I can't tell Marie about those if I'm to convince her of my intentions with Matthew.

"It seems like he's only using your unstable emotions against you to get what he wants."

"But he's my friend and it's not like we're kissing or fooling around." Not anymore.

"He's not treating you like a friend; he's treating you like a plaything. He's warming you up to later make you do something you don't want to."

That hurt. Is he really that bad? Am I letting him use me? Thoughts swirl inside my mind and I feel dizzy. Marie stays silent to let what she said sink in.

"I wish you had known Mattie from before. He'd skip out on football with all his guy friends to go wandering through the woods with me looking for a castle. He'd pretend to be my knight in shining armor escorting me away from all the dangers in the world."

"I didn't realize how close you two were. I'm sorry, Katie, but sometimes sweet boys grow up to be jerks. He might be sugar-coating it but he's not being sweet."

"I thought he would have told you about us growing up together after the first time I brought him to the room. I thought that's why you were okay with him after that."

Marie's brows scrunch together. "When would he have told me that? The only times I've seen him is when he's with you."

"No, the very first night. You made him leave then I went to work. When I got off work, he was waiting for me and he said he went back to talk to you and that it was all okay now."

"Katie, he never came back to talk to me." Her eyes grow wide with worry.

I begin to feel panicked and think back to that night. "No, he had to. He said you told him where I worked, that's how he knew where to find me."

"I wouldn't tell a stranger your whereabouts. You should know that. I think he knew where to find you because he's stalking you. He was hanging outside your classroom the day of your Calculus test. Not a cute waiting but more of a possessive one."

I let my mind swim, trying not to drown in the conflicting thoughts. Is Marie, my best friend, lying about never having talked to Matthew in hopes I stop trusting him? Or is she telling the truth and my childhood crush has turned into a lustful monster biding his time?

On unsteady feet, I stand and walk to the bathroom. I run

cold water and throw it into my face. I take deep breaths and focus on calming down. My hand begins to slide into my pocket. Maybe another finger prick will help clear my thoughts.

Before I can get the blade out, Marie changes the subject and calls to me from the room, "I never did ask, did you get your Calculus test back yet?"

"No, the professor said he should have them graded by the end of this week so I should get it back tomorrow."

"Well, when you pass, you and I are going out to celebrate. No guys allowed." I hear her light giggle as she attempts to bring us back to normal. "Oh, hey! I almost forgot. I bought a new movie if you're up for it."

I walk out of the bathroom and see Marie push the disk into the DVD player under her small TV that sits on a shelf built above her desk. She flashes me the case featuring a girl glancing teasingly behind her at a guy dressed in a suit. "What is it?" I stroll to her side of the room and slip under the blanket on her bed.

"Some cheesy romantic comedy that we'll both hate. I'll make the popcorn."

We settle in leaning against the wall and each other munching on the big bowl of extra buttery popcorn. The movie starts with the main characters being polar opposites meeting by chance with the predictable foreshadowing of them falling in love.

"They always make the men in these movies such jerks before the woman comes along. Why can't there just be nice guys for nice girls?" Marie throws a piece of popcorn at the screen.

"I think I'm doing the opposite to Scotty," I mumble to myself.

"Are you two okay? I mean, he doesn't know about Matthew yet, but is there something else going on?" Marie turns to me with her full attention though I wish she wouldn't.

"I guess. The other day he became angry over something little. That's why I've been afraid to say anything about Matthew. Scotty and I are doing great and I don't want to mess it up by telling him I have a new guy friend."

"I'm sure it's not you that made him angry. Things at home have been rough on him and school is probably stressing him. Maybe you could go visit him this weekend"

"Yeah. Maybe. I don't know." I bring my knees to my chest and bury my face.

"Katie, every relationship has its ups and downs, but if you're on a down it doesn't mean you have to branch out." I wish she would stop bringing this back to Matthew.

"I'm not trying to! I only want to be Matthew's friend like when we were kids. He just makes it so difficult." I watch the credits run up the black screen.

"Maybe try giving yourself some space. Try working through things with Scott. Take a break from Matthew until you work everything out and are thinking clearly. Then when you do talk to him again make sure he knows you don't want that kind of relationship. You can tell him that, and if he doesn't want to be just friends then he's obviously not the same as when you were kids." Marie climbs out of bed, turns off the TV, and puts her disk back into the case.

In this moment I think about telling her everything. I want to tell her about Scotty's jealousy, about Matthew's kisses, about the weird conversation I had with Mom on the phone last week that won't leave my mind, about the losing battle I'm having with my own emotions, about dancing on the precipice of self-harming.

The words form on my lips but then freeze. If she doesn't like Matthew now, what would she think if she knew I kissed him? If she knew how fragile I really was becoming would she think I was a freak? Would she become too motherly or distance herself? If she knew all the things about me from the past few weeks would she still treat me the same?

The desire to confide in her disappears like it was never even there.

CHAPTER EIGHT

Sitting on my bed, curled into a tight ball, I stare down at my Calculus test I just received back. 59%. F. This is the second test I have taken this semester, and although a 59% is better than a 34%, it's still an F.

My dark thoughts encircle my body in a heavy invisible blanket that tries to squeeze my lungs and choke the air out of them. In one big wave of emotion I feel myself crashing. I'm letting everyone down. Why can't I control my grades like I want to?

My grades have to be above average, no questions asked. My scholarships are what allow me to go to college. Without them, I would be a burden on my parents with expensive student loans.

But I'm going to lose those scholarships because I can't understand Calculus.

As I hear Marie unlock the door, I hastily try to wipe the smeared make-up off my face and crumble a tissue in my hand to press my new bleeding fingertip into. As she walks by, she glances at me and tosses her backpack on her bed.

"Hey, girl." Her cheery greeting is usually welcoming and contagious but not today.

"Hey."

"How'd you do on your Calculus test?" Reminded of my failure I can't stop the tears from coming again. She rushes over to my bed and pulls me into her arms. "Aww… Katie, don't cry. What's wrong? It is as bad as the last one?"

I nod and nudge the test toward her. She picks it up and flips through it.

"Well, at least you improved a little. Maybe next time you'll improve some more." She gently strokes my hair trying to comfort me and calm me down.

"Why is this so hard for me? I've always understood math but this... this makes me feel so stupid." I drop my head back into my knees.

"You're not stupid. You just need some help. Have you gone to see a tutor?"

"Yes, once a week for the past month." I don't lift my head, so the words come out muffled.

"Have you talked to the teacher? Or how about joining a study group?"

"I talked to the teacher and he put me into a study group with some of his best students."

"How's that going?" she asks in a hopeful voice.

I lift my head to level my gaze at her. "I'm so confused at what I'm doing. The group started planning the studies when I'm in class or at work so I can't make it to them."

"What? That's messed up!" She shakes her head and goes to pick up her keys from her desk. "Come on." She takes my hand and pulls me from the bed.

"Where are we going?" I walk to the mirror and take in my disheveled look.

"To the one place that I know will make you happy." She smiles and brushes through my hair as I re-apply mascara to my lashes.

"You know, my shift doesn't start for another hour."

"I know but you like to be early and you can show me all the new additions and we can play with the puppies before you have to work."

"Playing with the puppies is my work."

"Well, then ask for overtime!" She starts to giggle as we walk out into the hall.

Marie blasts her radio with a country song and rolls down all her windows in her sporty silver Mustang. Before we turn onto the main road my phone buzzes. I motion for Marie to turn down her music and answer before the call times out. "Hey, Cassie. What's up?"

Heavy sobs fill my right ear and she chokes out a response, "I can't… can't make it stop…"

I cover my left ear with my hand to block out the rushing sound of the wind as I realize the seriousness behind the call. Marie rolls up the windows to help. "Make what stop? What's wrong?"

Several seconds pass before Cassie can pull herself together enough to talk. My heart pounds in anticipation but I don't push her. I hear her take a deep breath, collecting herself. "You said don't let the bad ruin the good, but there's too much bad. The voices don't stop. Even when I sleep, they're in my dreams. I can't make them stop."

"What voices?"

"They're in my head. They keep telling me how unwanted I am. That's why I go to so many foster homes, why I don't make friends, why I lost my brother. No one wants to be around me longer than they have to be." The sobs start again.

I will my voice to come out strong. "Cassie, listen to me. You are not unwanted. There's been circumstances behind some of those foster homes that I'm sure had nothing to do with you. And your brother is probably out there tracking you down as we speak. I'm your friend, and once you begin to settle in with this new family, you will make other friends. I know it must be hard always living in change, but change can be a good thing. It can create a new and stronger you."

"Will the voices stop?" Her voice sounds younger than her sixteen years.

"They'll stop when you make them. Those voices are your self-doubt." I hold up my index finger to Marie as she parks and turns her car off letting her know I'm almost finished. When Cassie doesn't answer right away, I proceed cautiously. "Maybe you should think about talking with a therapist. Adjusting to an ever-changing life can be unsettling, and they may be able to help you."

Cassie takes a few more deep breaths and I can hear her fighting the tears. "You're starting to sound like everyone else. I'm sorry for bothering you."

"I've told you before, you're never a bother. I'm want to help."

"You're trying to tell me I'm crazy and send me to someone else because you can't help me!" She ends the call and I sit motionless. I fight the urge to call her back immediately. She needs some time to calm down. I can call her tonight after work and try again. I can figure out how to help her.

I don't know how when I can't even help myself.

I shove the dark thought away. Marie sits patiently and I give her a small smile. "It's Cassie. She's been stressing a lot while I'm away."

"Poor girl. I couldn't imagine moving around so much and not knowing which family will always be there for you. But I think she really looks up to you, even though she lashes out. That's how most sisters are."

"I'm an only child. I don't know how to be a big siter to

a girl I've only know for two years." I stare out the car window at the traffic.

"I think you're doing just fine. She called you when she needed help. That means she trusts you. She'll come around." Marie lays her hand on my arm and I turn to face her again. Maybe she's right. I take a deep breath and exit the car.

As soon as I walk into JoJo's Jungle my mood instantly lifts. Marie was right about one thing; this is exactly what I needed. We walk over to the dog kennels and sit in front of them. As we open all three cages a mixture of puppies fly through the openings and shower us both with wet, slobbery kisses. The speeds of their tails echo their excitement of being free. They clamber around over our laps and run at their full potential through the shop.

Joe walks over from behind the counter with a small smile on his face. "A bit early today, aren't you?"

"Yeah, I've had a rough day and needed some animal time, and Marie wanted to visit before she had to go to class."

"I'm sorry to hear you had a bad day. And hello, Marie. How are you?"

"I'm great! Just being eaten by puppies!" She giggles and Joe offers his hand to help her to her feet.

He then pulls me to mine and looks around. "You know you have to put all these pups away if a lot of customers come in."

"I know. I'm moving them to the pen now." I scoop a tiny Yorkie off the floor and plop him in a tear down pen I suggested for near the door. This way customers can pet the dogs and watch them play, while the dogs get a little exercise. Marie follows with a fluffy black Pomeranian.

"I know you do." Joe looks almost sad but before I can ask him if anything was wrong Leo comes out of the back carrying a large cardboard box and Joe hurries over to hold the front door for him. I push the thought away for later and continue grabbing puppies.

"So, what's new here?" Marie asks as she looks all around the store after setting the last dog in the pen.

"Well it doesn't look like we have anything new from this week. Actually, it's really cleared out in here. They must have made a lot of sales while I was off yesterday."

"Oh well, that just means there's plenty of room now for new animals. I hope they get some more rabbits soon. Those things are so darn cute!" She walks over to the rabbit pen and pets one of the few remaining ones.

"Of all the exotic animals in here you like a plain old rabbit." I laugh to myself.

The bells on the door ring as a customer walks in and I click into work mode. She looks around appearing lost, so I walk up to her. "Can I help you with something?"

Her shoulders relax and she smiles, grateful for my offer. "I sure hope so. My son asked me to pick up some crickets for his bearded dragon. He usually comes in to get them himself, but he's been feeling sick, so I volunteered to pick up some, but I have no clue what I need."

I smile. "That's okay, I'll get you a couple dozen to give to your son. They're only a dollar a dozen."

"That's great! Thank you so much!"

I begin walking to the back room where we keep the crickets and feeder mice. Marie calls out to me from the door, "Since you're working now, I'm going to get out of your hair and head to class. Do you want me to pick you up tonight when you get off?"

"No, I close so I'll have one of the guys drop me off." I wave and start bagging crickets.

CHAPTER NINE

As my shift begins to wind down, I look out the window into the night. The street is empty like the shop. I love working until closing. It's usually when the guys are in the best mood and when the joking really starts. Half the time I end up in some cage with an animal. It sounds mean but it's all in fun.

I finish sweeping my pile of dirt and dog hair into a dustpan and put the broom away. When I walk to the counter, instead of being greeted with laughter, it's uncharacteristically quiet. Joe opens the cash register and hands me an envelope.

"What's this?" I open the envelope to find a few twenty dollar bills.

"It's your pay for this week." He doesn't look at me when he answers.

"But it's Friday. You have always paid on Mondays." I go to hand the envelope back, but Joe shakes his head.

"You won't be working here anymore after today."

"What?" For a moment my thoughts fly apart. What have I done wrong? I go through everything in my mind that I've done today. Nothing stands out as wrong but there must be something. Something worth firing me over. I was being fired, wasn't I?

Joe, Leo, and Dwayne just stand silently. What did I do?

"Is this because I let the puppies out?" It's an irrational thought but right now I am irrational. "I mean, I only did it so they could get some exercise, I feel sad that they're caged up all the time, but I don't have to do that anymore, really, I'll leave them in their cages and -"

"Katie, calm down." Joe's voice is soft and level like he's rehearsed that very line a hundred times.

"How can I calm down when you're firing me, and I have no clue why?" Tears form in my eyes, but I refuse to cry in front of these guys.

"I'm not firing you. Katie, we can't keep the shop open here anymore. It's become too expensive. There are not enough people here to buy things to equal the expenses of keeping the shop open. I'm going to Baltimore where my brother lives. He told me about a building for rent for the shop and he is going to give me a place to stay until I find my own."

Through all this I stay quiet, unbelieving. I look at Leo and Dwayne. How are they not upset? This is all they do. What will they do without the pet shop? I look back at Joe. "Who's going to work for you if you don't have us?"

Joe takes a deep breath but before he can respond, Dwayne speaks up, "We're going with him."

"What?" For the second time tonight, the air rushes out of my lungs and my brain stops working properly.

"Katie, we swear it's nothing against you, but we don't have anything tying us here, no college, no family, no other jobs. Other than a few friends, including you, we won't be leaving much behind. Joe is really going to need us."

Leo walks over and throws his arm around my shoulders. "We hate leaving you, but you have school. You're going to do great things with your life. Don't let this bring you down.

It's not like you'll never see us again. That's what breaks are for, long car trips. "

"How can you guys do this?" The tears slip out now and I can't help but act petty. "Don't you see what this place means to me? I come here all the time, even when I don't have work scheduled. This place makes my bad days better. Look at today. I had a bad test in Calculus. I was so upset but as soon as I got here, I felt so much better. I forgot all about it." Until now.

I try to think of an alternative. I'm majoring as a veterinary technician because all my life I've wanted to work with animals, but who says I need a degree to do that? Finding this job has shown me it's everything I want. I allow myself to think of the possibility of going with them. Would having a job make the disappointment of dropping out of college less drastic for my family? Would I be seen as a failure? Even as I play with the idea in my mind, I know I couldn't do it. My life is here. Here with my parents and Scotty. I couldn't imagine packing up and leaving them behind.

Joe watches the waves of emotions filter across my face. "We know how much you care about this place and the animals here. And I'm sorry to hear about your test." He pauses to dig out a pack of tissues from behind the counter and hands them to me. "But we're not making money here. We're losing money. We can't stay open if we don't have the money to take care of the animals."

"But this is my job. I need the money. Isn't there something else you can try?" I try to grasp at anything I can to change his mind.

Joe gives a sympathetic smile. I know he can see right through me. "You know I don't pay that much. You were never here for the money. There are other places in town that are hiring, and they can pay you more than I could. And, if it helps, you can come help us pack. We're closing next week to the public but seeing your face will make it a little less somber."

"I can come help, but a new job won't be the same." I know I sound whiny but it's not fair.

"I know." Joe comes from around the counter and wraps his arms around me. It's strange. He's never been a comforting type to me, but I collapse into the embrace. "The shop won't be the same without you either." We stand in silence for a long time. I try to process everything that is happening, but it only makes me feel sad. Joe finally moves to switch off the lights. "Do you want us to drive you back or is Marie coming to pick you up?"

"I think I want to walk myself back." My voice is flat, and I feel empty.

"We can't let you do that. It's dark and that's dangerous." Dwayne fishes his keys from his jacket pocket.

"No, I'll be okay. It's only a mile to campus. I'll send you a text letting you know I made it back. The fresh air will help clear my head." And I need the solitude to relieve the growing pain inside that is threatening to tear me apart.

Reluctantly, he puts his keys back. "Alright. Don't forget to text and be careful."

"I will." I hug each of the guys in turn. I am really going to miss them.

Once out the door the full force of my day hits me. Things are happening too fast. I walk along the quiet street wondering what I've been afraid of all this time. The sound of my lone footsteps on the sidewalk along with the distant traffic on main street is the only thing piercing the night. Previous fears of a mugger emerging from a shadows and holding me at gunpoint doesn't even bring goosebumps.

I slip into the darkness of an alleyway and pull my pocketknife out. I know this is becoming more frequent and that I should stop, but it seems to be the only thing that can reign in my out of control emotions. They've never been this strong before.

I prick the tip of my left ring finger. The skin has grown increasingly sensitive in the past few weeks from meeting my knife point so often. My emotions appear numb to the pain, so I press harder. Still nothing. I pull the blade downwards creating a small cut. I felt that.

A new idea comes to me. I pull the sleeve of my hoodie up past my elbow and look at the soft flesh of my forearm. I place the blade against my skin and pull it down toward my wrist. I watch the blood run down my arm after I move the blade away. I wince but it doesn't hurt that bad. Mostly it feels like the cap of a shaken soda popping off. I take a couple deep breaths. Things are going to be fine. I am in control.

I pull a tissue from the packet Joe gave me and wipe the blood from the new cut.

CHAPTER TEN

Once back in my room I throw myself on my mattress. Marie sits propped up on her bed, typing on her computer. She looks over at me in my collapsed state. "Hey, Katie, tough day at work?"

I sit up and give her a halfhearted smile. "Yeah, it was different today."

"How so?" She asks with a casualness, but I feel backed into a corner.

"Umm… it was more work and not really much joking around." I strategically keep my eyes averted from her gaze by texting Dwayne informing him I was back in my room.

"Oh, well at least you had animal time. You needed it." She grins, appearing proud of herself for being able to help.

"Yeah, it's been nice being at the store," I mumble, and Marie goes back to watching the screen on her lap. She doesn't hear the underlying message in my words. She doesn't know that work didn't relieve my stress but added to it. She doesn't know that my stress relief isn't there for me anymore.

My decision to not tell her was last minute. I don't want

to drag her into another one of my downward spirals. I don't want her to have to take care of me like I'm a helpless child anymore. All I want is to talk to Scotty. He'll know what to say to make me feel better.

I try to wait patiently, squirming to get comfortable, knowing he will call any minute. He always does. I reach for my phone and as I'm about to speed dial him my phone lights up and plays the chorus to Collide by Howie Day.

"Hello?" My voice comes out a little too anxious, but I can't deny I'm happy to hear from him. Marie has her headphones on and the sound up so loud that I can hear it, so I take advantage of her distraction to stay in bed.

"Hey, Katie." His voice is soft.

"You couldn't have called at a more perfect time Scotty." I begin to arrange my long overdue story in my head.

"Why? What's wrong?"

"I've had an absolutely terrible day." I try to mentally prepare myself to tell him all the things I've been keeping to myself for too long.

"Yeah, I did too."

"Really? Wow that's strange. I'm sorry, Scotty." I take a deep breath. Here goes nothing. "Mine started when-"

"Wait. You're not going to ask about my day? Are you not concerned at all?" The sincerity in his voice from earlier is completely gone, replaced with pure malice.

I am momentarily shocked at this wave of anger from him. "I... yes I was going to ask. I just thought I'd tell you about mine and get it out of the way then listen to yours."

"You can be so self-centered sometimes. You know that, Katie?"

"What? Why are you being so hateful?" Why is he speaking to me so condescendingly? I know he's been having these moods lately like I've been too emotional, and I should try to calm him down, but I have no control over myself.

"I'm being hateful, am I? Because I want to get some stress of my chest? Just forget I asked what's wrong. I'll call back later. Bye, Kathryn."

"Good -" The phone clicks, "bye...?"

What just happened? Why is he so angry? Why am I so emotional? What is wrong with me? What is wrong with him? I thought we were doing better since his last outburst.

Something serious must have happened to him today to upset him so much. I need to apologize when he calls back and try to get to the bottom of this.

As soon as I lay down my phone there's a knock at the door. I know exactly who it is, and as much as a part of me wishes it wasn't him, another part of me, a new part that doesn't seem to think straight and that I don't really understand, is glad he's here.

Marie looks up from her computer, sighs, then slides out of bed. I guess she can hear with the sound up that loud. She gathers up her computer and her phone and heads for the door.

"Marie, you don't have to go. I'm not running you out of the room." I try to reassure her to stay but she levels a look of disapproval at me. It's a look that I'm beginning to see more and more.

"Yes, I think I do, Katie. You need to figure this out. I keep my opinions from him for your sake, but I have my limits. Ever since Matthew came back into your life, you're not acting like yourself. The Katie I know isn't a liar or a cheater. He's changing you, and not for the better."

I know she's mad and I know she doesn't approve of this, I don't even approve of this, but I can't stop.

She opens the door and steps around Matthew. He flashes her a smile. "Where's the fire, speedy?"

She ignores him but yells back to me, "Text me if you need anything," That's Marie. She's angry but she still cares.

Matthew shuts the door behind her and walks over to my

bed. His unruly brown hair falls in his eyes. They're green for now. I follow his cheek bones down to his mouth that is almost always fixed in a half smirk.

I still don't know why he appeals to me as much as he does. When he's around all my grounded down-to-Earth thinking goes out the window. I'm hypnotically drawn to him against all my better judgement.

He climbs onto the bed and pulls me onto his lap, and before the reasonable part of me can protest, his lips are on mine, soft but persistent.

Finally, he releases me, and my lungs struggle for air. That's the way he is, capable of making me breathless with just one kiss. "How was your day?" He nuzzles my neck.

"What are you doing?" I push him back so he can see my face.

"You seem tense," he says simply as he grazes his lips against my collarbone.

I slide off his lap and put a few feet of distance between us on the bed. "I asked you not to kiss me anymore. I thought you were okay with just being friends."

"Middle school is over. No more of this BFF game. It's time to grow up." His voice is matter of fact, but my ears hear the words much harsher.

"So, you've been toying with me? All our talks have meant nothing?" I'm not going to cry. I'm not going to cry.

"I didn't say that, but it was all getting a bit boring, even you must agree?" He lounges against my stacks of pillows as if waiting for me to come back into his arms.

"They weren't boring to me, and I have questions. I didn't want to ask them because I was afraid of the answers but now that I know how you really feel. I don't see why it should matter anymore." I feel brave.

"Fire away." Matthew studies his fingernails, unamused, which only fuels my anger.

"I don't even know where to start. How about, did you talk to Marie like you said? Or why do your eyes change color, because I don't remember them doing that when we were kids? What subject are you even studying because I've never seen you in class, or going to class, or doing homework?" I piece together the real question, but it comes out in a quieter voice. "What are you?"

"That's enough questions, Katie Cat." His voice drips with danger.

"I told you not to call me that." I slide back on the bed again until my back hits the wall.

"Aw, come on, don't you know how attractive it makes you sound?"

"I'm not attractive without a pet name?" I know I shouldn't care what he thinks. I know he shouldn't even be here with me, especially acting like this, but I can't make him leave.

"Oh, you look pretty good to me." He looks at me hungrily and I watch as his eyes mysteriously change from green to silver once again. I stare at them and he must take my silence as acceptance, because he grabs me and pulls me onto him again, kissing my neck. His mouth moves along my jaw and then stops at my ear to whisper, "Let's see if we can make this kitty purr." He nips at my ear lobe as he pushes me back onto the bed, climbing on top of me.

All my anger and accusations slip away as his mouth and hands continue to explore and I sigh his name. It feels like I am no longer on Earth, that I am no longer a part of this life. Everything else is gone and it's just him and I. I have no thoughts of my failing grades, lost job, or stressful phone calls. There's no room inside.

But then I hear something. It's faint but familiar. As I focus on it, the sound becomes louder. It's not just a sound, it's a song. I sit up quickly, knocking Matthew back mid-kiss.

It's Scotty's ringtone.

CHAPTER ELEVEN

"No, no, no, no." I frantically search for my phone in the ruffled comforter.

"Just don't answer it. Come back up here with me." As inviting as Matthew sounds, a part of me wakes up and knows I'm in the wrong here with him.

"No, he said he would call back. I have to apologize and figure out what happened to him today." The ringtone stops and my heart drops. I throw all the pillows off my bed and finally find it. "Mattie, can you come back later? I really need to talk to Scotty now. There's something wrong and I have to tell him about you."

"I'm not going anywhere. You're with me right now. He can wait."

Anger heats my face. "Matthew, I'm not kidding. Can you please leave?" I point to the door. The phone in my hand starts to ring again and my stomach sinks. I can't miss his call again. What will he think? "Fine. Just don't say anything."

"Yeah, sure." He waves a dismissive hand, but I choose to answer the call before it times out instead of pursuing his unconvincing compliance.

"Hey, Scotty. Sorry I didn't answer, I couldn't find my phone."

"It's okay, Katie. I want to apologize for earlier. I'm not sure why I snapped at you the way I did, I guess I was really stressed from today. I didn't mean to upset you."

I smile to myself. I knew he wasn't really mad at me. "It's ok. I'm sorry too. I should have asked you about your day instead of getting caught up in mine."

"It's not your fault. I don't know, it's like someone turned up the angry dial in my head. I had no reason to be that angry. I don't know where it came from."

"I said its okay. I don't need an explanation. Do you want to tell me about your day now?"

Matthew snorts a laugh rather loudly. I glare at him and he smiles innocently back batting his lashes.

"Sure, but what was that noise?"

"Oh, uhh... I didn't hear anything. What kind of noise?" Matthew's smile widens almost like a lion looking at the mouse it has been toying with.

"It sounded like a laugh. I don't know. Anyway, Mom and I got into a fight this morning."

"Oh no. What about?" I stand up and move to Marie's side of the room hoping Matthew takes a hint.

Matthew laughs a little more plainly.

"Okay, I know I heard something that time. Is Marie in the room? Or her boyfriend? It sounded like a guy laughing."

My heart rate quickens and cold sweat beads form on the back of my neck. "No, I'm here alone."

"Yeah, right." Matthew doesn't even try to speak quietly.

"Who is that, Katie?" Anger starts to drip into Scotty's words.

"No one, Scott. Tell me about your mom." I'm desperate to diffuse the situation unfolding around me. I think about hanging up and calling it an accident after I kick Matthew out but I'm afraid that would seem more suspicious.

Before I can uncover a solution from my cloudy thoughts, Matthew speaks again, "Look, Scott. She doesn't care about you or your mom. She's with me tonight so beat it, okay?" Matthew has moved from my bed to stand right behind me. I twirl around and stare at him wide eyed.

Scotty's fury snaps me out of it. "Katie, who is with you?"

"Scotty, he's just a friend -"

"A friend you had to lie about?"

"Scotty, no, I just haven't found the right time to tell you about him. I didn't want to make you upset -"

Scotty continues to interrupt me before I can calm him down, "Upset? Why would I be upset about some guy sleeping with my girlfriend behind my back?"

"He's not sleeping with me!"

"Yet." Matthew walks back to the bed looking at ease.

"Shut up, Matthew! You need to leave." I force so much anger into my words that I don't even recognize my voice.

"Fine. I can take a hint. I'll see you soon." He winks then strolls out the door as if nothing is wrong and I wish my eyes could burn holes in the back of him.

"Scotty?" My heart is thundering in my chest.

"I'm done, Kathryn." The anger is gone but the empty dead tone is worse.

"What does that mean?"

"It means I'm done. Done with this relationship and done with you. I can't be with you if you're going to lie to me and cheat on me and whatever else it is you're doing."

"Scotty, no. Please?"

"I can't do this anymore."

"Scotty…"

The unmistakable sound of his phone click fills my ear. "Scotty?" I am too shocked to put the phone down until the screen lights up signaling the end of the call. I sit incredibly still, unbelieving of what just happened.

An hour passes and still nothing. No tears came to streak my face. I feel numb.

He can't leave. We always talk our way through our problems. Even as I think it, I know this time is different. I think of the finality in his voice.

Mechanically, I slide on my bedroom slippers and Scotty's jacket over my clothes. Once out of the room. I walk with no destination in mind. A few guys run down the hall yelling and laughing about something. Typical Friday night behavior.

But this isn't a typical Friday night for me. Normally I'd be on the phone or video chatting with Scotty but not tonight.

Or any night ever again.

I make my way down the stairwell and open the outside door on the ground floor. The cold surrounds me and the wind bites into my underdressed body, but I don't care. I can't really feel it.

Still walking without thinking I find myself making my way toward town. I cross the main road and think, just for a moment, of staying in the middle for the road. One of the large eighteen wheelers would deafen my ears with its horn and squealing breaks, but it wouldn't be able to stop fast enough. I shake the thought and keep walking. There is a bridge that connects Keyser to Cumberland; a bridge that overlooks the Potomac River; a bridge that I now find myself standing on.

I don't know why I'm here. I keep hearing Scotty's voice, "I can't do this anymore," and then the phone click. The first tear quietly slides down my cheek as the realization hits me.

I have never felt this low. Looking back at the events leading me to this moment, I don't know if my feelings are irrational because of stress or if this is how it feels to want to end it all. Everything has pushed me to the breaking point.

How did things fall apart so fast?

I knew my grades in Calculus weren't good after the first test, but the end of the semester is approaching faster than I thought and I am running out of time to fix it. My GPA will be too low for some of my scholarships. College is slipping from me.

The pet shop, my safe haven for stress relief, will soon be gone as well.

And Scotty… he's already gone. I ruined our relationship. What had I seen in Matthew? How could I have let him lure me into this? I was so happy with Scotty. I wasn't even looking to find someone like Matthew. He just came in and swept me up into his chaotic world. Something in him pulled me in, almost as if I didn't have a choice.

But I did have a choice, didn't I? And I chose wrong. So now I'm paying for it. Cars fly by behind me on the highway, uncaring of my late-night unraveling. If I was gone, there would at least be less stress on everyone else. Scotty wouldn't have a cheating girlfriend, my parents wouldn't have to try and find college money, Cassie could find a friend who could actually help her, my roommate wouldn't have to take care of me like a child.

The more I dwell on it, the more the ache in my chest intensifies until it is unbearable. My tears begin to flow chaotically down my face. I look down over the bridge into the empty black void. I keep fighting for control over my own life, and I keep failing.

There's one more thing I can try. I roll up my sleeve and retrieve the pocketknife from my jacket pocket. The long cut up my arm looks irritated and angry. I push the blade into my skin and add a second one. The blood flows as I make the cut deeper. Crimson droplets dot the cold cement ground beneath my feet.

I wait several minutes, feeling dizzy from the blood loss,

but the relief doesn't come. The pressure doesn't release. Zipping my jacket up to my throat, I take a step forward. I shake my head trying to get rid of all the thoughts swirling inside.

But I fail.

They swarm, trying to consume me. All the failures, mistakes, and losses threaten to suffocate me. I can see only one way out. One way to control what happens to me here and now. I step closer to the short ledge and swing one leg over.

Then the other.

Sitting there I take one last deep breath and whisper, "I love you, Scotty"

Then my hands shove me forward into the darkness.

PART TWO: SCOTT

CHAPTER TWELVE

It's been almost a week since they pulled her from the Potomac River. It still feels like I'm dreaming. Time is passing, but I'm frozen.

What have I done?

Her funeral is in a few hours. Mom laid out my suit and keeps giving me comforting pats on the back, unsure of what to say, but she doesn't know that this is my fault. No one does.

How can I go and face her parents? Oh, yeah, I'm the reason your daughter killed herself, my condolences.

The thought of never hearing her voice or never feeling her kiss again, threatens to break me down. But I refuse to cry. I did this, and there's no way to take it back.

Thinking back on the night we broke up I can't find an explanation for why I became so angry. I know I was upset because I had a stressful day and was anxious to get it off my chest but snapping at Katie the way I did was out of line. Maybe it all built up and turned into a blind rage. I still don't understand who I became that night. But no matter the why's or how's I know it's irreversible.

But my thoughts keep returning to the male voice on the other end of the phone. Who was with Katie? Was he really just a friend, or did my instincts know something I was afraid to say? Is that why I became so angry? Or was I being irrational and not giving her a chance to explain? It hurts more not knowing.

Dressed in the suit, complete with a black tie and black shiny dress shoes, I slide into the driver's seat of my truck and try to take deep breaths to calm my chaotic nerves.

What have I done?

She had her whole life to live. College was going great, her job made her happy, she had a wonderful family, and she had me to love her. Had. But then I took it all away. I ended her world.

Where is she now?

When I pull into a parking spot at our small church, I don't get out of the truck. I don't think I can do this. My hands are shaking, and tears threaten to come again. I feel so weak and I hate feeling weak. I open the door, get out, and slam it shut with more force than I need to.

When I walk into the church only a few eyes meet mine, but no one comes to offer me comfort. I suppose that's how it should be. What am I? Just a boyfriend. Right now, her family needs the support.

Walking up the middle aisle, I look from one grief-stricken face to the next. There's a mix of people; her family, teachers we had in high school, friends, church members, they're all here for her. Did she not see how many people loved her?

Sitting in chairs next to the front pew are her parents. Daniel has a dry face, but he looks beaten down, while Jackie lets the tears flow. I walk toward them, unsure of what to say.

Daniel sees me first and nods. I nod back. When Jackie looks up to see me, she stands and throws her arms around my neck sobbing. Shocked by her actions, I gently but awkwardly pat her back as she mumbles things like, "I'm sorry," and "Why did she leave us?"

I don't know what to do or what to say. Of course, I knew Katie's parents, but I never spent much time with them. This affection is unfamiliar, but I know it is only sorrow driven.

Once she calms down enough to let me go and sit back down, I walk up to the front of the room. Katie's casket is closed. I can't decide if that's harder or easier for me. I had hoped to see her one last time, but I don't know if I could have handled seeing her pale body lying in a casket. So peaceful, but so still. Every hue imaginable fill one bouquet or another as the flowers adorn her casket and overflow from the alter.

In an attempt to distract myself, I look at the poster boards that show her life in pictures. There are older photos from when she was a baby and all her school ones. A large image shows her standing proudly on a stage accepting her high school diploma. Some pictures are of her that someone got from Facebook and some are her with her family.

Surprisingly, there are even a few pictures of her and I. One photo is of us at the homecoming dance at her college, and another is of us decorating her dorm room. Looking back, it's hard to understand what I was thinking a week ago.

What have I done?

The funeral begins and everyone takes a seat. I slide in a stiff padded chair next to Cassie. She stares off without acknowledging my presence. I know she looked up to Katie. I can't imagine how she must feel. I reach out to touch her hand, but she snatches it away.

"I told Katie everyone always leaves, including her," Cassie hisses.

"I think this is a little different than someone skipping town." I try not to let sarcasm dip into my voice. She's hurting, so she's lashing out. Isn't that what I did?

"I know. I just don't know what to do. I was a jerk to her the last time we talked. I was waiting for her to call me back so I could apologize, but she never did. I guess I know why now, but it's worse. She died with me upset with her. I can't fix that, and it sucks." Cassie angrily brushes the tears away and goes back to staring at nothing.

"I'm sure she knows you weren't really mad at her. Katie was good about seeing the best in people." My words don't affect Cassie, at least not in a way that I can see.

The preacher steps up to the alter and begins the typical "she was too young, but it is in God's plan" speech. Thankfully he keeps it short. Then comes story time. It seems everyone in the room has a story to share of a time Katie helped them do something or made them smile.

A pause hangs in the air and before I realize it, I'm rising to my feet. "I have a memory to share too. A memory of the day my whole world changed."

I walk to the front of the room and try to ignore all the stares. A few people nod expectantly while others dab their faces with tissues. One face catches my attention for a moment. He sits in the back in black jeans and t-shirt with a dry face and a bemused look. He watches me as if waiting for something, but I ignore him too. I close my eyes and think of the first time I met Katie.

It was a cold day in late winter in the middle of our junior year. I had recently moved here and didn't really know anyone yet. I was walking home from the library when I decided to pop into 7-11 for something to drink. I fixed up a cherry Slurpee and as I was paying, I noticed a girl sitting at one of the outside tables.

She was bundled up in a purple sweater and a rainbow hat with one of those fluffy balls on top. She wasn't facing my direction, but I wasn't watching her face, I was watching her hands. She stared off into space as her hands mindlessly dropped Skittles into her bottle of Dr. Pepper. She did it in such an absentminded way that I could tell she'd done it many times before. I walked outside to her table and pulled out the chair across from her.

"Is this seat taken?"

She looked stunned and her eyes shifted as if she was looking for a direction to run, but then she shook her head quickly. I sat down and started to drink my Slurpee. She didn't relax even after I looked at ease.

"Why do you do that?" I gestured to her drink.

"I just like the flavor." Her voice was quiet.

"It must be good. But I've never seen anyone do that before."

"No one else is weird like me." A hint of a smile played on her lips.

"I don't know. I just might be weird enough to try it." I smiled, and she relaxed a little. She slid the bottle of soda toward me. I grabbed it then hesitated. "You're quick to share. What if you're trying to poison me?"

"You're as weird as me by wanting to try my drink. Why would I poison you? You're someone I'd like to keep around as long as you like my drink."

We clicked instantly after that and a week later I asked her on a date.

After all the stories are shared the group of people move outside to the graveyard right behind the church and we stand around a gaping hole in the ground. A hole that will soon swallow up the one thing in life that I had once said I loved more than life itself. How did things happen so fast?

Its early April, but the sun beats down on me. Its warm rays feel so out of place. Today is sorrow-filled. How can it be sunny? The rain should be hammering down, pouring like the tears of the people who surround me.

As Katie's coffin is lowered into the dark earth, grief's

iron grip takes hold of me around my throat and I can't breathe. I bolt away from the group. Halfway back to my truck, I have my head bowed, and bump shoulders with someone. I look up to apologize, but the words are lost in the silvery eyes looking at me. The guy smiles a broad grin and takes my hand. "You'll see her again soon." Then let's go and walks away.

I unfreeze and run back to my truck and before I can stop them the tears come. I scuff my shoes in the gravels as heartache flows heavily down my face. I try closing my eyes but all I see is her. I hear her laughing and I clamp my hands over my ears trying to block it out, but it doesn't do any good. My breath becomes ragged as the memory of the last time I heard her voice enters my mind.

"Scotty, I've had an absolutely terrible day."

She had a terrible day? I wish I knew what had happened to upset her that much, but I was stupid and didn't even give her the chance. I was consumed with my own stress over Kevin, the arrogant snob from my school that was supposed to be my partner for a sculpture project in one of my classes. There is no common ground between us and absolutely no cooperating. He pushed me as far as I could go until I snapped. I punched him in the middle of class. I was dismissed for the day, but I don't regret it.

However, my actions did get reported back to my employer. I'm a campus activity coordinator and good conduct is a requirement for the job. After a long talk I ended up keeping my job, but I lost my hours for the week.

The biggest problem I faced that day was my mother. I am an art major, so my ideas of important classes are those art related, but my mother thinks differently. I'll admit, my English grades could be better, but they're not my main objective. She lectured me for two hours on how I needed to do better and try harder and get my priorities straight and blah

blah blah. It was the biggest fight we've ever gotten into, especially since we've pulled together so close since Dad left.

Anger surges through my veins and pushes my heartache out of the way. I stand up from my crumpled state and slam my fist into the side of my truck. The blow leaves a dent and my knuckles are bloodied. The pain shoots up my arm, but it doesn't matter. I open the door and get in. Buckling my seatbelt doesn't even cross my mind. Gravels fly as I spin out of the church parking lot. Speeding down the road I know I'm driving way too fast, but I don't care. I want to outrun this. All of it. I want it all to disappear. I don't want to think about Kevin, or Mom, or Katie. I push the gas pedal down closer to the floorboard and cut the turns as sharply as I can. A reckless feeling takes over me.

I could escape it all for good. The next turn I approach at high speed. A guardrail hugs the road to create a barrier from the steep bank on its other side. Coming into the turn I jerk the wheel, but this time the truck jerks back. For a breathless moment there is nothing, no time, no sound. I am flying.

The last thing I hear is an ear-splitting crash.

CHAPTER THIRTEEN

At first everything is too bright, but the air is warm and a freshness so pure drapes over me in comfort like a cozy blanket.

When the world starts to come into focus, I find myself staring up at a man.

He is cloaked in a white robe with a golden sash and matching golden sandals. Huge white soft feathery wings extending from his back shimmer in the sunlight and floating above his head is a solid gold ring.

A halo. An angel. I'm dead. And.... in Heaven?

"Hello, Scott. Peace be with you. My name is Michael." His full brown beard spreads up the sides of his face to his head where his hair falls back down to his shoulders.

"How did I get here?" My thoughts slowly return to me as my eyes flit around trying to see everything at once. Behind Michael stands a large impressive gold gate. An actual golden gate. It doesn't connect to anything, no fence or border. Just the gate sitting open and inviting. Leafy green trees and bushes dot the grassy field resembling a park.

"You died in a car accident."

I feel a twitch of anger brewing inside. "You and I both know it wasn't an accident. I wanted to wreck. To disappear for good. But Katie. I hurt her. I don't belong here."

"Of course, you do. Our record keepers never make a mistake. The guilt you put on yourself for Kathryn's death is irrational."

My focus snaps back to Michael's face the moment he says her name. His silver eyes stare into me. "Then who is to blame? I'm the one who broke her heart right? Pushed her over the edge? Surely you must know that since your record keepers are so perfect." I let the malice drip into my mouth and coat my words.

Sounds like you were given too much anger to handle. It will soon be replaced with peace and joy." Michael shakes his head as if I was a small child that asked a silly question.

My irritation grows as he ignores my argument. "Did she make it to Heaven then? Or was she deemed unworthy by your corrupt sounding system?"

"She's here." His gaze wanders past the gate, across a lake, and rests on a small table with a bright red umbrella shading it. I take an unsure step in that direction, but Michael throws his arm out stopping me from proceeding. "She doesn't know you anymore."

Unwillingly I pull my gaze from Katie and level a glare at Michael. "What do you mean she doesn't know me anymore? What did you do to her?"

"It's part of entering the Kingdom. All memories that are linked to dark emotions; sadness, anger, jealousy, greed; are erased, so you can begin a new life here. One full of only happiness. There are no dark emotions here and no way to stimulate or provoke them once you've entered yourself."

"You brainwashed her?" All the heartache and anger from life apparently followed me into death and I can't control it any longer. I swing my fist toward Michael's face, but where the impact should be there is only air. I stumble forward as the momentum throws me off balance. Michael's hands catch my shoulders and I steady myself. My back now faces the gate and I glare skeptically at the creature before me. I should have hit him. We're standing so close. No way I missed.

"There is no violence here either." His constantly calm voice is starting to annoy me. "And we did not 'brainwash her. We gave her peace."

"And what the hell is that supposed to mean?" My fists clench at my sides.

"I've already told you. Those dark emotions were tied to the memory of you, therefore that memory is gone."

"So, it is my fault she killed herself. You just confirmed that. So, you lied to me. I didn't know lying was allowed in Heaven." I cross my arms and give him a smug look.

My retort doesn't faze him. "I did not lie to you. There are more reasons for why she ended her life. I did not say you were not one of them, only that you are not the only reason."

"Sounds kind of deceiving to me. What other reasons? Tell me because I'd love to know I'm not her executioner." Despite my efforts to hide it, the curiosity slips into my voice. Ending the way we did I never found out what happened to Katie on the last day of her life.

"Maybe you should have asked her that yourself when you had the chance."

That stung. That was a slap in the face with a mace dipped in lemon juice.

Michael smiles at the discomfort he's caused. "It does not matter. Once you cross into the Kingdom, your memory of her will be gone as well."

"Yeah? And what happens if I don't want to go into your corrupt Kingdom?" I put Katie through hell, so that's where I should be.

"Everyone crosses into the Kingdom."

I plant myself where I stand. "Well that stops now. I refuse. Send me to Hell or back to Earth. I don't care, but I can't stay here where she and I could be sitting across from each other and neither of us will remember the love we shared."

"You would still have that love together on Earth if you hadn't been so selfish."

I throw my hands up. "Whoa, whoa, now you're judging me? I don't think it's your place to judge me. Isn't that God's job? Where is he? I want to talk to him about this."

"Pass through the gate. God is in the Kingdom." Michael's voice hovers over impatient but his face stays calm and relaxed. All except for his eyes. I didn't trust him for the angry gleam his eyes aren't hiding so well anymore.

"Can't you ask God to come here? I've always read that he is kind, patient, and understanding. I'm sure he'd help me if I asked. Being brainwashed isn't something I've read in the Bible before, so I'd like to have him explain this to me."

"That's out of the question. You won't see him, but you will pass through the gate." Michael takes a step toward me. I refuse to accidentally step back too far so I stand my ground but not easily.

"That sounds like a threat. I thought there was no violence here?" I begin to feel very uneasy. I have no idea what Michael can do to me since I'm already dead, but I don't want to find out.

"Once you pass through the gate all acts of violence will be forgotten."

Before I can question him or object again his hands spin me around so that I'm facing the gate and the meadow behind it then he shoves me so hard I stumble forward.

CHAPTER FOURTEEN

For a disorienting moment, I blink rapidly and look around. Behind me, Michael stands smiling. Part of me wants to smile back, but another part of me that doesn't make sense decides not to. So instead, I turn away and continue taking everything in.

The world before me is open. Vastly open. A giant meadow with the most lush, green grass sits in the middle of the rolling hills that stretch out as far as I can see. Here and there are deer and rabbits grazing among people on picnics. There are buildings placed sparsely about. Some look like little stone cottages and others look like shops with tables dotting their lawns.

In the middle of the meadow is a lake. Its water refracts the sunlight like liquid diamonds. Out on the calm waters are all kinds of boats holding people who are laughing, reading, or simply relaxing.

On the far end of the meadow are tables topped with brightly colored umbrellas. People sit at them, licking at ice cream cones or sipping on drinks. While glancing at the unfamiliar faces my eyes land on one girl. She sits alone, gazing out across the meadow away from my direction. She absentmindedly drops Skittles into an open bottle of Dr. Pepper.

My mind is suddenly jerked into a memory. A memory of a world that is less bright and less peaceful. A similar scene is before me, except instead of a sunny meadow, I am standing on a sidewalk on a street lined with shops. Cars fly by on the road behind me and people bustle in and out of doors bundled in heavy jackets. The girl that now sits in front of me is faceless. Her blonde hair blows in an imaginary wind in such a way that masks her identity. But her quiet voice speaks clearly to me.

"I just like the flavor."

As quickly as I was pulled in, I am thrust out of the memory.

Shaking my head, I try to call back the image, but I can't see it as clearly as I had the first time. I don't know the street I had been on and I can't place the girl, but the connection between them suggested something. I just don't know what.

I look back at the girl at the umbrella table. She still isn't looking in my direction. I have a strange urge to talk to her, but I don't even know how to start that conversation.

Oh hey, you remind me of this girl in a weird flashback I had but can't remember. Nice to meet you. Want to be friends?

Frustration feels foreign inside of me, like it shouldn't be there. I turn back to Michael for help. "Who is she?" I look in the direction of the girl.

"Her name is Kathryn."

"How did she get here? She's so young." I don't even remember how I died. Car crash?

"She drowned. But she has no memory of it. It was a tragedy."

"Her death would be a tragedy no matter how she died,"

I mumble that more to myself than to Michael but then in a bit louder voice I address him again, "Can I talk to her?"

"Of course. This place is meant for socializing. Especially here in the meadow."

I nod and start walking around the lake. The sun is pleasantly warm, not hot, even though from the height and intensity it should be scorching out. A soft breeze blows gently through my hair and all around me. It's quiet here other than the sounds of light conversation and laughter.

As I near the umbrella tables a man comes out of one of the shops with a platter full of doughnuts. He's short and pudgy, probably ate too many of his own pastries, and he has a full graying beard. "Welcome to the Kingdom! Have a doughnut! What's your name? I'm Jacob!" He shoves the platter toward me and talks too fast.

"Umm... I'm Scott." I pick one of the sticky treats from his tray and give him a half smile. "Thanks."

"Oh, you're welcome! Just remember I always have fresh goods here at my bakery!" He waddles off, popping a mini muffin in his mouth as he goes back into the shop.

I look back at the girl, this time she's looking at me, but as soon as her eyes catch mine, she looks away. She must be shy. I approach her table. "Kathryn?" Her name is sweet on my lips.

She looks up at me. Her warm brown eyes have an innocence to them that I'm sure was restored when she entered the Kingdom. "How do you know my name? Have we met?"

"I'm not sure if we've met. I don't remember much of my life, but Michael told me your name because I asked." I pull the wooden chair out across from her and take a seat.

"Why did you ask about me?" Her eyes widen. The simple shine in them reminds me of a baby deer's hiding in the grass waiting for its mom to come back.

"I was curious. You seemed familiar and I wanted to talk

to you." I break my doughnut in half and offer her a piece.

She accepts the treat but then softly shakes her head. "Familiar? I'm sorry but I really don't remember anything. Michael said I had a rough life before I died so he erased the memories so I could be happy here."

"Doesn't that seem unfair to you?" I put my elbows on the table and lean in a little.

"No. It's nice to have no worries and to only be happy." She licks the sugar from her fingertips which look extra red, but I can't see why.

I level her a skeptical look. "Are you happy? You're sitting here alone with Dr. Pepper and Skittles."

She looks down at her candy filled drink and blushes. "I know it's weird but-"

"You just like the flavor, right?" I finish and she looks at me in awe.

"How did you know? Do you do this?"

"No, but I think I knew someone who did." I lean back in my chair and try to recall who, but I can't.

"Well that person has good taste." A ghost of a smile plays on her lips. I smile too and we both relax. "And I am happy here, I'm just not much of a social butterfly."

"You're as pretty as a butterfly." As soon as it's out, I want to take it back. It felt like such a natural response but I'm definitely going to scare her away.

For an uncomfortable moment she sits there probably unsure what to say. To my relief, she brushes it off. "That was very cheesy, are you like that with everyone you meet?"

"Definitely not..." My voice trails as my brain begins going somewhere else at jet-like speed.

I'm no longer sitting at an umbrella table. I'm in a bedroom. It's dim, only lit by strings of rainbow lights. The girl from my first flashback stands in the middle of the room. The same ghost wind keeps her face hidden behind her hair.

Somehow words form in my mouth without me thinking them. "You have a lot of rainbows."

The girl looks around. "I think rainbows are beautiful."

I take a step toward her and gently cup her face with my hand. "Not as beautiful as you"

"You're so cheesy."

I feel myself leaning forward but then it all fades away too quickly. I again find myself sitting in front of Kathryn who is looking at me with a raised eyebrow.

"Umm… Are you ok?"

"Yeah, I uhh… I'm fine. I blanked out there for a minute." I rub my eyes as if wiping sleep away. Death is just a deep sleep, right? Is death living forever in a dream state?

"No kidding."

"Sorry." We let the silence drip in. Kathryn sips at her soda while I try to decipher the strange visions I'm having. I don't want to mention them to her because I don't want her to think I'm crazy.

"You haven't told me your name." Her gentle voice brings me out of my thoughts.

"It's Scott."

"Scott. That's a nice name. You can call me Katie if you'd like. What do you think of this place?" She sweeps one arm around, gesturing to the whole meadow.

Her attempt at small talk is cute and a smile takes over my face. "Well what I've seen is beautiful. I especially like the lake. But what about Michael? What's your opinion on that guy?"

"Michael is a wonderful angel. He's so generous to share this perfect life with us." She sounds so sincere.

"Really? I thought he came off as a bit arrogant. Like, 'Oh look at me, I'm head angel'." I wave my hands in a mocking way.

Her brow furrows. "That's awful. I don't see that at all.

He's so kind."

I drop my arms. "Maybe there's two Michaels? Like a good cop bad cop thing?"

"I don't think so." She's shutting down. I need to save this conversation. It feels too right talking to her for it to end. I start to look her over, as discreetly as I can, trying to find a topic. She's wearing a plain white, button-up shirt and blue jeans. In her hair, holding her bangs back, is a rainbow clip. None of that suffices for the long conversation I'm craving. I begin to look for tattoos or jewelry, anything that can tie her back to her old life. Maybe I can learn who she was and if I really had known her before.

Katie extends her arm to pick up her Skittles. Her sleeve pulls back and I look at her arm for a bracelet, still desperate to find something. Instead, I see cuts. Two deep red lines that begin at her inner wrist and slice up her arm beneath her sleeve.

What has this girl been through?

The question sends my mind back in time. I can't get used to the whiplash of being pulled into these memories.

This one is different than the last two. Instead of being in an unknown place with an unknown girl, I am standing here in the Kingdom with Michael, and I feel confused.

I'm looking at a girl across the lake. "Who is she?"

"Her name is Kathryn."

"How did she get here?"

"It was a tragedy."

Suddenly, I'm thrown back further in time. Michael still stands in front of me, but now I feel angry.

"Maybe you should have asked her that yourself when you had the chance."

I'm thrown back further to before I entered the Kingdom. I'm in my old room and I'm on the phone. On the other line a soft voice speaks with tears in her words.

"Scotty, I've had an absolutely terrible day."

Rage takes hold of me and I slam the phone down. In the same instant, that same rage propels my fist towards Michael who now stands in front of me again. I start to fall until his hands catch me and shove me forward through the gate.

The impact of hitting the ground jolts me back to reality. My hands slam onto the table to catch myself from the fall that was no longer happening. I feel my eyes widen and struggle to catch my breath, but when I see Katie giving me a strange look, I try to compose myself.

I take a deep inhale. "I'm very sorry. I'm not myself for some reason today. I keep going off into space."

"It's ok, but I think you should go get some rest. You're starting to worry me." She stands and grabs her drink and candy. "Have a good day, Scotty."

As I watch Katie walk away, I ponder the name choice she made. Scotty. That's what the girl on the phone in my last vision called me. Was there a connection? Or was it only a coincidence using a convenient nickname? If so, then who was the girl in the visions? The one who loves rainbows and likes Skittles in Dr. Pepper? It has to be Katie, doesn't it?

The more I try to piece it together, the more confused I became. Why would Michael push me? And why am I having flashbacks? What does it mean? My head hurts. I guess I can ask Michael for answers if I ever see him around. But right now, I shove all the visions to the back of my mind. I'll figure it out later.

CHAPTER FIFTEEN

With Katie gone, I don't know what to do with myself. There's a wooden sign next to the umbrella tables pointing me in the direction of town. I look down. I'm in a suit. It's the same suit mom made me wear for graduation. I should try to find some other clothes. I wonder how money works here. I know I don't have any but maybe I can trade my suit.

I follow the dirt path, shaded by colorful blossoming trees. A couple of girls wave as they pass by. Smiles illuminate their faces and I find it effortless to smile back. In a few minutes some shops come into view. Their single-story stone structures create the simplistic vision of the village.

I walk into a clothing shop and begin browsing through some t-shirts hanging on the racks. The brands range from Hollister to Walmart and everything in between. "Howdy stranger." The clerk approaches me and says with a thick Southern accent. She's in her mid-twenties and has strawberry blonde hair tied into a loose braid hanging over her left shoulder and freckles on her cheeks. "My name's AJ. Is there anything I can help you with?" Her pale green eyes sparkle with excitement.

"I need some new clothes. This suit isn't very comfortable." I flex my arms in the constricting fabric for emphasis.

"Well, that's understandable. Most newcomers stop in here for a change. Take anything you like." AJ gestures around the shop.

"Take it? You mean it's free?"

"Why of course! Money doesn't have any purpose here. That's why it's always so peaceful-like." She gives me a soft smile and walks back to her counter to talk to some other people.

I turn back to the clothes rack. With everything always free I can pick out a change of clothes now and come back tomorrow for more. Then it hits me. It hadn't crossed my mind until now, but I don't know where I'm supposed to stay.

I walk up to the counter with my clothes. "Excuse me AJ. I have a question to ask you."

AJ looks back over at me and smiles. "Sure, what do you need?"

"How do I go about getting a place to stay for the night? Is there a hotel or something around here?"

"Oh, that's easy! No hotels, but if you ask any of the angels walking around, they will show you to your new home." She points out the shop's open front door to the path outside.

"Oh, thanks. And thanks for the clothes." I turn to leave.

"Anytime sugar. Come back when you need more."

I nod and head back outside. It doesn't take long to find an angel. He's dressed in similar clothes as Michael and the impressive wings are hard to miss. When I approach him he smiles. "Hello, child."

"Hi. I was told if I asked one of you angels, you'd take me to my house?" Do I really get my own house?

"Certainly. I didn't realize you were new. Welcome to the Kingdom, I'm Jeremiah."

"I'm Scott."

"Nice to meet you. If you'll follow me." He begins walking. "Your house is down this street here, six houses down. I hope everything will be to your liking."

"I'm sure it will be perfect." We walk in silence past five other houses. Their structures are similar, but their unique styles widely vary. One has a large impressive stone entrance, while another is mostly made of glass and looks more modern. It doesn't take long to reach my house. Jeremiah hands me a key. The picture-perfect log home is surrounded by a small yard. Nestled beside it is a pond with a stone bench placed on its bank.

I walk up to the front door and unlock it. When the front room comes into view, I am speechless. Every piece of furniture in the room looks to be vintage art pieces. All the tables are even crafted out of sculpting clay. The walls are swirls of blue and yellow, replicating Van Gogh's "Starry Night". It's an artist's fantasy.

Over by the window is an easel and a wide variety of art materials. I walk over to it and run my fingers over the assortment of paint brushes. "All this is mine?"

Jeremiah chuckles. "Of course. It's a standard house but we try to design them around each individual's own personality and interests. I assume you approve of the choices we have made for you?"

"Oh, I approve alright!" My face stretches into a wide smile as I feel like a child on Christmas morning.

"That's good to hear. I'll leave you to yourself then. If there's anything you need, we have left some instructions in the kitchen for you and if there's something you no longer want just leave it outside your door." I nod and he turns to leave. "Have a good day, Scott."

"Thank you."

Ten minutes after I hear the door shut behind Jeremiah, I still cannot believe what I am seeing. This room is amazing. Then I remember I still have the rest of the house to see.

I walk through every room. I have the living room I came into that also has a large map on one wall, a bedroom with a king-sized canopy bed, bathroom, kitchen with a small table and two chairs, and two spare rooms that have not been decorated. I guess I can choose what to do with those.

In the kitchen I look in the refrigerator. It is fully stocked with my favorites from chocolate milk to blueberries to butterscotch pudding. It's a bit creepy that someone knows so much about me down to these small details but then again, they are angels. I look in the cabinets and find a box of snack cakes. I grab a pack and sit down at the table.

There's a white envelope with a golden seal. I open it to find a welcome letter along with instruction on how the magic works here. It says all I have to do is think about what I want, say it aloud, and it will appear. I can order about anything, including pets. Pets, huh? I've always wanted a pit bull. I conjure the image of a black terrier with a white chest and little white toes. And I say it? I look around and then back at the letter. "I would like an adult male pit bull." After I say it, I feel a bit silly but then there's a knock at my door. Did Jeremiah forget something?

I walk over and open it. There on my front step sits the dog I just ordered. I look around but there's no one in sight. This place is amazing! I lead my new dog into the house. He's a handsome boy with the iconic blocky head and big expressive brown eyes. I wonder if he belonged to someone in the living world.

"What am I going to call you?" He looks at me and wags his nub of a tail. I head to my bedroom and change into the black shorts and blue t-shirt I just got at AJ's store. "How about Lobo? I think it means wolf in Latin or something." Lobo jumps up on my bed and curls up. "Yeah, I'm ready to get some sleep too."

I crawl into bed and flip out the lights. I start to think about what all I've been through today, at least what I'm allowed to remember of it. I haven't had one of those visions since Katie left. I wonder if there's a reason for that. I try to piece it together, but exhaustion wins out and I'm soon asleep.

CHAPTER SIXTEEN

I remember everything.

This morning when I wake up, I don't have foggy memories that are out of reach. I have it all. Crystal clear. I remember crashing my truck, I remember talking to Michael and what a jerk he was, I remember my last phone call with Katie.

Katie…

I remember her. I remember everything about her and everything we had and everything I lost.

Does she remember me?

Better yet, does she hate me for being so angry that night?

I have to find her. If our memories are coming back to us, I need to talk to her before she thinks about it too much. I don't want her to be alone and upset.

I go to the large map on my living room wall. It has the whole town on it and streets twisting around its borders, but I can't find names on any of the houses.

In the corner there is a plaque that says, "Say the name of who you are searching for and picture them clearly in your mind."

My eyebrows scrunch together. I sigh. "Kathryn Taylor." Right before my eyes a street leading from the small square representing my house lights up. I trace along it with my finger until it stops in front of another square.

That must be Katie's. The magic here is weird like it's in my mind.

I copy down the directions on a piece of paper and walk out the door.

In town people are everywhere doing everything: talking, shopping, eating, and walking to the meadow. The odd thing is everyone I see looks to be around my age except for the occasional older or younger person. Maybe the angels arranged us that way so we would be around people we were similar too. Perhaps there are towns with only babies or old people.

When I turn up Katie's road, I get a sick feeling in my stomach. What if she won't talk to me? I was awful to her…

I shake my head. I can't think like that. I have to stay positive. We can fix this. I know we will have to talk about the guy in her room that night, but one obstacle at a time. This time, I'll listen.

When I reach the tenth house on the street I stop and stare at it. The yard is decorated with a vast array of flowers. Animals scamper through them uncaring of my presence. The pond beside her house is identical to mine except it is dotted with ducks, swans, and geese.

The house itself is a mismatch of colors. The siding is sky blue, the roof is red, the door is pink, and the shutters are lime green.

This is definitely Katie's place.

I take a deep breath to calm my nerves and walk up the porch steps to the front door. I knock lightly then step back to wait. It only takes a moment for the door to open and there's

Katie.

She's wearing a white sundress with a rainbow belt. Her hair hangs free in waves over her shoulders. Three black kittens romp with each other around her feet.

She smiles warmly at me. "It's nice to see you again, Scott. Is there something I can help you with?"

That's not quite the greeting I was expecting but nonetheless I'm happy to see her again. "No, I was just wondering if we could talk?"

"Of course. Please come in." She stands back and opens the door for me. As I walk into the house more animals come into view. Two German Shepherd pups are playing tug-of-war with a chew toy. A large orange tomcat stretches from a nap on the sofa. A few colorful birds fly in circles above my head. "Are you feeling better today?"

"Yeah, much better, thanks…" My voice trails off as I watch a squirrel climb a tall floor lamp.

I look back at Katie who is watching me take it all in. "I really like animals," she says as if she needs to give an explanation.

"I should bring Lobo over for a play date one day," I say as Katie leads me to her kitchen and I sit at the small table. The room is bright with sunlight streaming through the windows and reflecting off the yellow walls and sunflower decor. It reminds me of her mother's kitchen back when we were alive.

"Lobo?" She asks as she reaches into a cabinet above the sink.

"Yeah, he's my pit bull."

"Oh, he'd probably love that." She heats some water in a kettle and brings a plate of sugar cookies to the table. She takes the seat across from me and nibbles at a one of the baked goods. "What did you want to talk about?" She pushes the plate toward me, and I take a cookie.

"Well I was wondering if you remembered me?" I hold my breath hoping all this casual politeness is a ploy until she knows that I remember her as well.

"Of course, I remember you," she says, and my eyes widen. "We spoke yesterday at my favorite café in the meadow."

My eyes close and I hang my head. "No, I mean before that. Do you remember me from when we were still alive?" I probe.

She stands to pour the now hot water into the two mugs she got from the cabinet. She adds a teabag to each along with four spoonfuls of sugar. "I don't think so. Should I?" She brings the mugs over to the table and sits one in front of me then returns to her seat sipping at hers. She pauses and her face reddens. "Oh, I'm sorry. I probably made that way too sweet for you. It's a habit, I'm not sure why I did it to both mugs."

"No, it's fine. You've always given me four spoonfuls because that's how I like mine, the same as yours. I was your boyfriend, Katie." Will she remember if I remind her?

"Really? I'm sorry, I don't remember you at all." She looks apologetic but I'm not ready to give up.

"We met in high school our junior year. I was new and when walking home one day I noticed you put Skittles in your Dr. Pepper and it made me curious enough to talk to you."

"Are you sure you're not confusing the memory of meeting me yesterday with an old memory of someone else? With having suppressed memories here I'm sure that can happen."

"No, Katie. It's you. I know you. You love animals and you always wear at least one rainbow thing. And this kitchen," I gesture all around me, "it's decorated like your mom's, right down to that sunflower apron hanging over there." I am desperate to convince her.

"You could know that simply by looking at me right now.

My house is full of critters and I'm wearing a rainbow belt, and good guess about the kitchen." She isn't smiling anymore, and she eyes me cautiously over the rim of her mug with each drink she takes.

"A few weeks before you… died, it was our third-year anniversary. I took you to the town park for a picnic and then we watched the sunset from the dock. You were so happy." I recall the memory and try to project it into her mind.

"That sounds really nice, but I still think you have me confused…"

"Come on, Kathryn. Why can't you remember me?" I look at her pleadingly.

"I just don't. Michael says I won't remember anything that has to do with bad emotions so if I don't remember you then you must be linked to something bad so maybe you shouldn't be here." She stands and takes my mug to the sink even though I hadn't touched it yet.

"Katie, no. I remember you. Everything about us was good. That Michael guy isn't the saint you think he is. You need to trust me and remember!"

"Michael is an angel! And I don't know what kind of connection we had back on Earth but it's not here. I think you should leave me alone please." She's trying to stay polite, but her words are stern. I try to remind myself that she doesn't really know what she's saying and that she doesn't mean it, but her words still stab my heart.

I slide out of my chair and look at her. "Look, Katie. I'm sorry I'm pushing you. I'll give you some space, okay? See you around?" I walk to the front door but stop to wait for a response.

"Thanks," she says as she shuts the door behind me.

I nod to myself and drop my head to stare at my feet that are walking away from the girl I love.

CHAPTER SEVENTEEN

Bloop. Bloop. I sit on the bench outside my house and toss pebbles into the pond. Bloop.

What am I going to do? Katie doesn't remember anything about me, but I remember everything. I remember our relationship, our breakup, her death, and my death. I even remember Michael pushing me through that stupid gate when I got here. But what does it all mean? Why do I remember if I'm not supposed to?

I throw my handful of rocks down in frustration and stand up. I need some answers and I know who has them.

Back inside my house I stare at the map on the wall. "Angel Michael." Nothing happens. "Michael Angel." Still no streets light up. "Where does Michael live?" My voice begins to raise. I shove my feet into my black dress shoes that I forgot to trade in and trudge out the door.

I could probably ask an angel but am I allowed to know where Michael lives since the map won't show me?

AJ's shop is bubbling with chattering happy people. It takes all my willpower not to make a U-turn back out. AJ herself stands at the counter sipping on a lemonade. "Back so soon Scott?"

"Yeah, I need to trade my shoes." I gesture to the stiff ones scrunching my feet.

"No problem! If you don't want those anymore, you can leave them here for someone else."

I pick out a pair of Nike sneakers that are a bit more practical to walk in and head back to the counter. "Do you happen to know where Michael lives? I need to talk to him."

Instead of complying immediately, AJ eyes me wearily only for a second but then her smile mask returns. "I overheard some folks yesterday say they stumbled upon his house while out walking. They said they went north outside of town and there was this big black mansion at the base of a mountain. They turned around and came back of course, but my guess is that's Michael's place."

Of course, he has a mansion. "Thanks." I turn to leave.

"I wouldn't go snooping around. You should respect his privacy." AJ eyes me again.

"You're right, I'll catch him in town sometime."

"Sounds like a plan! See you around!" Her chipper voice follows me out the door.

That was really odd. It was almost like there were two completely different people talking through her. Maybe her real self was shining through. Why is everyone still brainwashed but me?

I start walking back through town, but I realize I have absolutely no idea what I'm doing, but I guess I have this whole walk to come up with what I'm going to say. Wait. Am I going to talk to him? Or am I going to spy on him? That option sounds better since I don't even know where to begin on my ever-growing list of questions. He doesn't seem interested in sharing information anyway.

The bright sun beating down is beginning to annoy me.

Why is it so hot here? I take refuge in the shade of the forest. The farther I walk away from the town the denser the foliage becomes. Vines twist up and around the tree trunks and I have to take special care not to let the thick knee-deep shrubbery trip me up. There aren't any animals out here, at least none that I've seen. The quiet sits heavy on my ears.

All at once, I see Michael's mansion through the trees. It's black and eerie as it hides away from everything. I decide to spy, and if I'm caught? Improvise on the spot. That usually works when Mom corners me about something like school or a speeding ticket.

I allow myself to think about Mom for only a second. She's one of the few people I really miss. I hate myself for getting in that fight with her the day Katie died. With all that was happening at the time we never did patch that up. I never did apologize…

I shove the memory away. I can't think about that right now.

I peak around the trees until I can see the front door. Do I walk in and hope no one is in that room? Maybe I should look through the windows?

Creeping closer, I watch the door but be sure not to step on any sticks or crunchy looking leaves because that always happens in the movies and that person is always caught minutes later.

When I'm a few feet from a window beside the door, I glance around one more time but then I'm suddenly plowed into by someone. My back slams into the ground and that someone is straddled on top of me holding a knife to my throat.

Once the black spots clear from my vision and my eyes adjust to the sunlight, I see a girl's face looking down at me with teeth bared. But then her expression changes to disappointment and something else. Annoyance?

"You're not an angel. You're just another one of the zombies." She stands up and closes her pocketknife. I sit up and rub my aching shoulders.

"Zombies?" As I look at my attacker the first thing that I notice is that she's short. Even looming over me now I know she's short. I'm not a giant or anything but if I stood up, she might be up to my shoulders. She's a year or two younger than me and has very tan skin. Her curly dark brown hair is tied back in a low ponytail. For as little as she is, she sure knocked me down good.

"Yeah, a brainwashed zombie 'cause you don't remember anything." She looks around still annoyed. "Look, I was hiding and now I'm not so I think you should run along and forget this happened before I get noticed." She starts to walk away but I clamber to my feet and grab her arm.

"Wait, I'm not brainwashed. I remember everything." Excitement flutters in my chest. I'm not alone!

She looks at me then at the mansion and again back to me. She scowls and pushes me forward into the cover of the trees. "Fine. If you remember everything then tell me how you died." It isn't a question. It's a demand. She's testing me.

"I wrecked my truck."

"Why?"

"I was angry at myself because I was at my… girlfriend's funeral and it was my fault she…died." Those words are harder to say than I imagined.

"Okay, so suicide isn't a shocker but that's some dark stuff and if you can remember that you're definitely not brainwashed." She doesn't show sympathy to the story itself just nods in approval.

"I told you."

"Okay well if you remember everything then why are you going to Michael? That's like suicide, no pun intended." She glares at me skeptically. She's small but she makes me feel

108

uneasy.

"I was going to spy on him to try and figure out why my girlfriend doesn't know me, but then you tackled me and now he probably knows we're both here."

"Doubt it. He and his cohorts are so absorbed in what they're doing it's made them unobservant. I've been here for days. And if that was you spying then I'm sorry but you're the worst spy ever. Why did your girlfriend kill herself?"

I flinch at the casualty the girl has in mentioning Katie's death. "That's none of your business. And I'm new at this spying stuff. What makes you the expert? And where did you get a pocketknife? We aren't able to order weapons here." I know because I tried after coming back from Katie's. It's my turn to interrogate her but she doesn't seem intimidated.

"Whatever you were buried with is with you when you wake up here." She answers coolly and shrugs as if it's obvious.

"You had a knife buried with you?" I stare at her in bewilderment.

"You're not the hunting type, are you?" she asks but I shake my head and continue to stare at her wide-eyed. She sighs. "Yes, I had a knife buried with me. Now shut up so I can hear if anything is moving." She closes her eyes and her brow scrunches in concentration. We stand in complete silence for a long time. Then suddenly her eyes fly open and she pushes me down behind a bush.

The front door of the mansion swings open and two angels walk out. They don't look around suspiciously. They just stroll by chattering about how there's no female angels. I glance back at the girl beside me and she mouths, "Told you."

We sit quietly for a few minutes until we're sure the angels aren't in earshot. Finally, she stands up from her crouch and crosses her arms, "If I didn't have to babysit you, I would have had them."

"So that's your plan? Attack any angel you see? That's real smart. Don't you think they'll notice when their own are disappearing? I mean, can they even die?"

"Do you have a better plan, Lover Boy?"

I cringe at the nickname. "My name is Scott. And no, but your plan seems like it's going to get us…"

"Get us what? Killed? I have news for you, we're already dead. And who said we were working together?"

"Well, I thought since we both have our memories and we both want answers two people are better than one."

"Not when you're the second person." Her attitude is really getting to me.

"Hey! Stop insulting me! If you don't want my help, I'll do this on my own, but if I happen to see Michael I'll be sure to tell him I saw you sneaking around here." I am completely bluffing but I need to know what she knows if I am going to have any chance at snapping Katie out of her trance, and so far this girl is the only other person who remembers other than me and I'm tired of feeling alone.

She narrows her eyes at me. "You're lying."

I return her glare. "Try me."

For a few tense moments it's a standoff but finally she breaks eye contact and begins walking back toward town. "Fine. We'll talk back at my house."

I blink a few times stunned. I can't believe that worked! I jog after her to catch up. "So, what's your name?"

"Amanda. And if you call me Mandy, I will not hesitate to cut your tongue out."

I clamp my mouth shut. I don't know if I believe her or not, but I know I don't want to find out.

CHAPTER EIGHTEEN

Amanda's house is a mountain man's paradise. All her furniture and curtains are made with camouflage fabric and her end tables sit on actual tree stumps. The carpet is designed to crunch under your feet as if you were in the woods.

"And you're comfortable living like this?" I sit down on the couch while she takes the recliner next to a massive stone fireplace ablaze with orange flames.

"Surprisingly these angels know a thing or two about interior decorating. I couldn't have designed this better myself." She runs her hand over the chair arm.

"Okay, so getting to business, tell me what you know about these angels and this place." I lean forward resting my elbows on my knees.

"Why should I tell you anything?" she asks nonchalantly.

"Because we're working together. That's how this works. We need to share what we know to come up with the best plan of action." Does this girl have trust issues or is it just me she doesn't like?

"Well, all I know is that stupid angel Michael pushed me

through the gate to nowhere when I refused to do it myself. Then my first day here, I was really fuzzy and then BOOM, the next day I wake up remembering everything again."

"Yeah, that happened with me this morning, but I went to visit Katie and she was still clueless. Why do we remember when no one else does?"

"I have a theory about that. Tell me exactly how you entered this place."

"Michael said some things that made me angry, so I refused to enter and then he pushed me through the gate, and I was brainwashed for a day." I recite the events, marveling at the similarities between our stories.

"Then that's it!" Amanda bolts from her chair to stand in her eureka moment.

I stare at her confused. "What's it?"

"I've been watching Michael as people enter the Kingdom. They always enter willingly." She lifts her chin triumphantly.

"I don't understand. So what?"

She plops back down in her chair. "Ugh. Don't you see the pattern? You and I didn't enter willingly, and we regained our memories. Everyone else entered willingly and they're still happy-go-lucky zombies."

"You really think that's the answer? Willpower?"

"What else could explain it?"

"I guess so. What else do you know?"

"I don't know anything else.' She looks away from me and I know she's lying.

"Yes, you do. When we were back at Michael's mansion you said it wasn't a shocker that I committed suicide and you knew that Katie did too. You're hiding something." I'm not stupid.

She gives me a hard look. "Clever. I guess you're not completely empty headed after all. I've been real busy ever

112

since I woke up two weeks ago. In addition to watching Michael welcome people and staking out his house, I've also been questioning people in town. It takes a lot of pushing but everyone that I've asked doesn't remember why, but they know they committed suicide. Every one of them." She lets that sink in as I sit quietly.

"So, you killed yourself too?"

"Yeah." She looks away not offering any elaboration.

"Why?"

"That's not the point. Don't you think it's odd that everyone here died the same way? And don't you think it's odd you don't know anyone except Katie? I mean I tried finding someone that I know who died." She points to her large map. "But according to that, he doesn't exist here."

I never thought about looking for someone I knew like my grandfather who died a few years ago. I had been focused on Katie. "So, we're… selected?"

"Looks like it. And almost everyone here is our age, except for a few, like that pudgy baker." She rolls her eyes at the mention of the overly cheery man.

I had noticed that this morning. "Is this the only town in the Kingdom?"

"As far as I can tell. There's nothing else on the map and no signs in town pointing to another town, just the meadow. And that's another thing, have you noticed everything is written out for us? All the signs and notes on how to get to places and how to use things. If you ask me those angels want us to stay content and not bother them with questions."

My decision to team up with Amanda is proving to be a very good one. She has been questioning the details that I have brushed off and now I'm seeing everything so differently. "This is bigger than I thought."

"Oh yeah, Lover Boy, you're in deep. You going to get cold feet on me?"

"Not a chance. I'd do anything to have my Katie back."

"Bleh… I don't know if I can handle being in this love story you're setting up." Amanda wrinkles her nose and sticks out her tongue.

"I just need her to remember me." Remember me so I can apologize and so we can be happy together like before.

"Well, maybe since you two knew each other before it won't be that hard. I've drilled different people in town with questions to try to make them really think but no one has cracked. But I don't know any of them personally like you know Katie. Since you share some of the same memories that might be the key to unlocking hers."

"That's probably the sweetest thing you've said all afternoon."

"Don't get used to it."

"I've already tried reminding her of things. I told her how we met and what we did for our recent third year anniversary. She didn't remember or believe me."

"Did you try showing her some physical proof?"

"Like what?" I rack my brain for something at the house I could show her, but none of it is connected to our Earthly lives.

"Something you gave her, or she gave you? Maybe actually seeing something will jog her memory."

I try to think of something. I twist the ring on my left ring finger absentmindedly until it hits me. "Our promise rings!" I jump up off the couch and take long strides to the door. "I have to go see her right now!" Before Amanda has a chance to reply, I am out the door.

My legs can't carry me fast enough to Katie's. The excitement plants a smile on my face so big that to everyone else I must look like an idiot, or maybe I look normal in this strange place, but I don't care. I am ecstatic.

I'm going to have Katie back.

And when I do then maybe we can sit down and figure out what is happening here. Or maybe I could be content with not knowing and live out this luxurious afterlife. As long as I have her, I could be happy anywhere.

Well, death did put a damper on my plans back on Earth. I was determined to be the best artist this century has ever seen. I was going to make a name for myself and be big. Bigger than Picasso or De Vinci.

But there's no chance of that now.

My steps have less bounce in them but with the promise of Katie soon remembering me, my spirits aren't down.

Once I reach her house, I bound up her steps and knock on the bright pink door anxiously. The door opens slowly, and it takes all I can do to resist pushing it open farther and scooping the beautiful girl in front of me into my arms.

When she sees that it's me, she stays mostly hidden behind the door. I can see her face and a sliver of her dress. "Um, hi, Scott. Did you forget something here this morning?"

"No, but I have something I want to show you."

"I really don't think that's a good idea. I think you just need to go home and please stop coming here." She begins to shut the door. There's no way she's getting away that easy.

I throw my hand out. "Katie, wait!"

"Scott, I want you to -" before she can finish, the two German shepherds that were playing this morning push through the crack in the door at full speed. They push the door out of Katie's hand, and she loses her balance. She takes a step to try to regain it, but I see that she is going to fall so I reach out to catch her.

She falls forward into my arms. She looks around, a little disoriented from the commotion, and then she looks at me.

Her warm brown eyes threaten to swallow me whole. I've always told her I get lost staring into them. She's so open and accepting that I swear they lead directly to her soul.

I can't help myself, "Katie…" I lean in ready to kiss her for the first time in what seems like centuries.

But the moment that I'm feeling, she isn't. "Scott, stop please." Her voice is almost begging. My heart breaks at the sound of it.

"Katie, I'm sorry. Here, look." I let loose of her and she backs away quickly. I hold out my hand to show her my ring. "See? I have the same ring as you. They're our promise rings. We got them for each other on our second anniversary." She looks down at the ring on her left hand then back at mine. I can't read her expression. "Do you remember now?"

Her hands tighten into fists and her face twists into a look that is trying to be angry but is really on the verge of crying. "You probably just ordered that after seeing mine this morning. Leave me alone Scott! I mean it! Don't come here anymore!" The tears she is trying so hard to hold back slip down her cheeks. She turns and runs into the house slamming the door.

I stand there unbelieving. It didn't work. She doesn't remember me. She never wants to see me again.

And she's crying. I made her cry. Again.

I rush to the door and knock feverishly. "Katie, please, open up please. I'm sorry. Katie, let me in. I was just trying to help you remember. I didn't mean to try to kiss you. Please, Katie!"

With my pounding and hysteric pleading, I fail to notice Amanda standing behind me. She tries to cup her hand over my mouth and pull me back, but I am too tall and too irrational to comply.

Then, I feel my feet being swept out from under me and my back hits the hard wood of the small porch. For the second time today, I look up at Amanda's angry face as she sits on top of me.

She grabs my face with one of her small hands. "Now

listen here you big baby." She points away from the house down the road from where I came. "Two angels are standing only three houses down. You are harassing that girl even if you're not meaning to and that's not something they'll tolerate here. Plus, if you keep shouting 'remember me I remember you' stuff that won't be pretty either. So shut the hell up and pull yourself together. We'll think of something else when we get back to my place. Now, come on." She gets off me and extends her hand down.

I look at Katie's front door, then back at Amanda. I take her hand and pull myself to my feet. She starts walking and I follow, trudging heavily.

In the most idolized hopeful place, I feel hopeless.

CHAPTER NINETEEN

The next day at Amanda's, I sit slumped at her kitchen table It's made of a tree stump with the middle carved out so a chair and legs can still fit under. I've been brooding since we left Katie's yesterday. Katie hates me. She'll never remember me or what we had.

Amanda sits in the chair opposite me trying to look at anything and everything except my face. Every now and then she pats my shoulder awkwardly in an attempt to comfort me.

I long for the closeness of another person. It's like a burning need inside of me. I feel so alone. Alienated. Amanda lays her hand on the table after patting me and without thinking, I reach for it. I lace my fingers through hers and the warmth of her palm clears my head a bit.

She tries to pull her hand from mine. "What the hell are you doing?" She looks at me as if I had stripped all my clothes off.

I know I should feel embarrassed and probably scared by how she is going to retaliate but I don't. I feel empty. "I'm sorry, I just need someone and you're the only one here."

She thinks about what I said for a moment, but then sighs and tightens her hold on my hand. "Fine. But if you try to kiss me, I will punch you."

I flinch, not from the threat but from the thought of kissing someone other than Katie. Are she and I even still together? Or am I supposed to move on and find someone else like Amanda? I look at Amanda. Her tanned skin is smooth and toned. Her dark eyelashes brush her cheeks when she blinks or looks down. She is pretty, I can't deny that, but could I be with her?

No.

I have to save Katie. She is living in a world where all her best memories have been stolen from her and she would not be okay with that.

I stand up but I don't release Amanda's hand. It still feels nice to have her near, even as just a friend. "Let's go."

She stands and lifts one eyebrow as she stares at me. "Go where? Hopefully not to my bedroom because I haven't really cleaned it ever and -"

"No. We're going to spy on Michael. I'm going to save Katie." I don't know if she was seriously thinking the bedroom was an option for us, but I don't want to ask.

"Well, that little experiment lasted a whole two minutes." She snatches her hand from mine and stalks past me to the door.

"It wasn't an experiment. I needed someone to help me calm down."

"Glad I could be of some use to you." She opens the door and motions for me to go out.

"It's not like that Amanda. What's wrong? Look, I'm sorry I held your hand. I won't do it again." I walk through the door and steal a glance at her. Is that disappointment I see on her face? Once outside standing on her porch, I turn and really look at her, but she has her I-hate-the-world look plastered on.

"Whatever, Lover Boy. What's the plan?"

If she wants to be like that, I'll forget the whole thing. "We're going to the mansion."

"You do realize the sun is setting right?" She looks up at the twilight sky.

I look up. It's getting dark, but it doesn't matter. "Haven't you noticed? I suppose death takes away human needs. I haven't eaten a meal all day and I'm not hungry. It's been a long two days and I'm not tired. I haven't even had to go to the bathroom. I'm going to the mansion tonight. If you want to stay here then do it, but I'm leaving." I turn and start walking toward town. It's not long before I hear Amanda's quiet footsteps beside me.

"You really lover her, don't you?"

The softness in her voice catches me off guard. "Yeah I do."

It grows quiet between us. We walk through town and begin our hike through the forest that will lead us to Michael's. The moon raises high in the sky and it finally begins to cool off.

I'm glad Amanda came with me. I enjoy her company even with her snarky comments and brash attitude. There's more to her than she lets on. I wonder if I'll ever know who she really is when she's not being the tough girl.

"Amanda, can I ask you something?"

"Sure," she answers absentmindedly.

"You said everyone here committed suicide, and I told you why I did it, I was wondering what made you do it?"

She doesn't answer right away. I think she is trying to figure out how to word it but then her voice hardens, and she coldly replies, "Maybe you should tell me what you did to Katie. You did say it was your fault she killed herself."

My non-beating heart freezes inside my chest. She couldn't have said anything more hurtful. The answer to my question must be more painful to her than I thought.

The appearance of Michael's dark mansion breaks the uncomfortable tension between us. "I need to get inside."

"You're crazy. If we get caught there's no telling what they'd do to us," Amanda hisses.

"You don't have to come, but I'm going in. The answers to whatever they're doing to Katie and the other people here, are in there." I slip out of the cover of the trees and creep toward the front door. Amanda doesn't hesitate to follow.

I turn to look at her, silently questioning her intentions.

"What? I can't let you go alone. You're the worst spy ever, remember?"

I fight the urge to roll my eyes at her. I'm thankful she came along because let's face it, she's right.

When we reach the door, I try the knob. To my surprise its unlocked. Of course, who would they need to keep out if everyone's brainwashed?

The room we enter is huge with two staircases on opposite sides leading up to the second floor. Amanda closes the door quietly behind us and takes the lead. I don't argue, but I stick close to her side. This place is really creepy. The wood of the walls, floors, and stairs is black. All of it. Making the darkness more prominent. There's very little furniture and our footsteps sound loud in the emptiness.

Amanda bends down and unlaces her boots. She pulls her feet from them and motions for me to do the same. Walking in our socks is much quieter and I am again glad to have her with me.

It doesn't take long for us to pick up voices in the quietness. We follow them down a hall off from the main room and find ourselves outside a metal door that is cracked open enough to peak through. Amanda squats down and I stand above her so we can both see inside.

Michael and another angel hover over a large control

panel. There's dozens of buttons and flashing lights. Above them are several TV screens all tracking the movements of different people. Hooked to each TV is a monitor measuring heartrate and something else that ranges on a spectrum of red to green.

The other angel is closely watching one TV in particular. It shows a young girl, about fifteen, who is huddled on the floor crying. Something about him seems very familiar.

"Michael, look here." He gestures to the screen and taps a few buttons.

Michael walks over from where he was watching another screen. "Yes, I'd say she's getting close."

"Let me go there and finish it. One heartbreak and she'll be over the edge." His voice tugs at a memory just out of reach.

"I was going to send Jeremiah for this one." Michael turns away, but the other angel doesn't accept his reply. He squeezes his hands into fists.

"Why would you send him when I'm clearly the best choice?" He swivels in his chair and I get a glimpse of his face. That's where I've seen him before. He's the guy I bumped into at Katie's funeral. "I've already brought in Erin, May, and Katie just this week! That's sixty altogether that I've added to your numbers."

Katie?

Michael turns back to the other angel, his face is angry. "You need to learn your place Matthew."

Matthew?

And Katie.

Anger seizes hold of me, and I reach for the door.

CHAPTER TWENTY

Amanda rises to her feet quickly and wedges herself between me and the door. She looks sternly into my eyes and shakes her head. I don't need her permission. I have something that needs to be settled.

I put my hand on her shoulder to push her aside but in one swift movement she pulls her pocketknife out and snaps open the blade. She glares at my hand and I snatch it away. I know she's crazy enough to use that knife on me and I need all ten of my fingers to wrap around Matthew's throat.

She shakes her head again as if reading my thoughts and points in the direction of the front door. I plant my feet on the ground as a show of I'm not going anywhere.

Her jaw locks tight and she points again. When I don't move for the second time her impatience shows on her face. She moves around me, and I feel the sharp point of her knife pressed against my back. She presses it hard enough that I know she's serious but not so hard to break skin.

Instinctively I raise my hands up, still holding a shoe in each, as a sign of surrender and I begin walking to the front door. She doesn't remove her knife until we are outside, hidden in the trees. The grass and leaves feel weird under my sock feet. The moment I no longer feel the point, I spin around, enraged. "Are you insane? Whose side are you on?"

"I should ask you the same questions! If I had let you walk in there it would all be over! They would know about us and you wouldn't be saving anyone!"

In the back of my mind I know she's right, but it doesn't matter. I have to get to Matthew and make him pay for whatever he did to Katie. Somehow, I know this is his fault. I didn't know that until now, but it makes sense. He was in the room with Katie the night she killed herself and he saw me at her funeral before I killed myself. He's the link. Somehow.

Amanda watches my face. She must see my anger evaporate because her voice loses its hard edge. "So, what is it? What set you off?"

I feel deflated, like a balloon that lost all its air. "The other angel, his name is Matthew."

"So is like a thousand other guys on the planet. What's it matter?"

"That's the name of the guy Katie was with when I called her right before we…broke up." The words are bitter in my mouth. I never told anyone we broke up. The news of her death came before I could come to terms with what I had done. Speaking it aloud feels like a lie.

"Ah, so the truth comes out. You and Katie aren't even together. You dumped her because you were jealous and then she killed herself."

"I had every right to be jealous! She was with him, but she lied and said she was alone. I didn't know it was a freaking angel with her!" I ball my hands into fists. Why her? Why did he have to come into our lives and manipulate her? And why was he at her funeral? Why did he tell me I was going to see her again soon? Did he know I was going to kill myself? Did he make it happen?

"If you were so sure she was being unfaithful then why

did you feel guilty and kill yourself at her funeral?"

"Because…" My voice trails off. I don't know. Why had I felt such strong emotions? Was it Matthew's doings or my own? Both when I broke up with Katie and at her funeral, I hadn't felt myself. Sure, I was angry, but that anger had been more. It had engulfed me and made me its slave.

"Look, Lover Boy, I want to figure this out as much as you do but I need to know if I can trust you to not let your hurt pride get in the way again, alright?"

I nod slowly.

"Okay, let's go back in."

We sneak back into the mansion and once again stand outside the room. Michael and Matthew must have resolved their argument while we were outside because now Matthew is sitting back in his desk chair with his hands clasped behind his head looking very pleased with himself.

Michael picks up a golden bracelet out of a basket of many identical ones. He tosses it to Matthew. "This needs to be done as quickly as possible. We need to have the numbers on our side if we are going to even have a chance at defeating the others. They may not be able to stop us here, but Earth is fair ground."

"And that's why you have me. I'll be back before you know it." Matthew slides the bracelet on his wrist and disappears.

I look at Amanda, my eyes wide. She glances at me and rolls her eyes then returns her focus back to the room.

Michael mutters to himself, "I have you because I can't do it myself." He then moves toward the control panel and watches the screen. The girl looks around as if she had heard something. She stands and opens her bedroom door. Standing there with a broad smile is Matthew.

Is he on Earth?

His wings and white robe are gone, replaced with a black

T-shirt and jeans. The girl hugs him tightly. I wonder what he said to her. There doesn't seem to be any sound.

"Oh, you're feeling love my little Jamie? Well let's turn that up." Michael turns a dial on the control panel and the heart rate monitor for the girl's TV speeds up. The arrow on the spectrum points well into the green.

What did he just do to her?

On the screen the girl kisses Matthew. He picks her up and walks to her bed. He leans over top of her and kisses down her neck.

"We can't have you feeling scared, Jamie. You need to get attached." Michael turns a few more knobs and the heartrate goes even faster and the arrow is all the way up on the green end.

As the girl gives in to Matthew, I find myself no longer able to watch the screen. Did he do that to Katie? Amanda must have noticed my change because she grabs my hand. I look at her and she gives me a sad smile. It helps a little, but I still have so many questions and uncertainties.

After a while I will myself to look back at the screen. The girl is wrapped in a blanket and sobbing heavily as Matthew looks to be laughing at her. The arrow points at the red section.

"Sadness, guilt, betrayal… good. Let's turn those up to an overwhelming high." As soon as Michael turns the knobs, the arrow drops to the lowest point in the red.

On screen Matthew leaves the girl's room and moments later he is standing in the middle of the room with Michael with his wings and robe back. "Piece of cake."

"I'm beginning to think you enjoy being with the humans. Feeling homesick?" Michael takes the bracelet from Matthew and drops it back in the basket where it came from.

"Not a chance. They're just fun to mess with, so naïve and desperate for love. I like being able to get something out of this plan of yours."

"Look." Michael points to Jamie's screen. She's stopped crying and her heartrate is slowed but now she has a pistol in her hand. She raises it to her head, and I look away. Amanda taps my shoulder and points into the room. I follow her finger with my eyes careful not to look at the screen. The girl's heartrate is a flat line.

She's dead. Just like that.

CHAPTER TWENTY-ONE

"I guess I should go to the gate and greet her. Why don't you go to town and act like an angel if you're going to wear the wings?" Michael's voice reminds me that I don't have time to be sad about Jamie.

Amanda and I scramble away from the door as the two angels walk toward it. There's another door across the hall and she opens it. It's a small closet but it's empty so we both squeeze in and shut the door just in time before the angels enter the hallway.

I crack the door and peak through to watch the angels walk to the front door. Amanda is packed so tightly against me I can feel her hot breath on my back through my shirt.

"The wings are badass. Plus, I've seen a couple lingering stares from the ladies." Matthew spreads his wings open wide.

"Sometimes you remind me of a kid playing dress up." Their voices carry down the hallway as Michael opens the front door.

"But I do it so well. Even your leader thought I was like you."

Finally, the front door closes shut with the angels' departure and I pour out of the closet. Amanda follows with her arms out in a stretch. "Well that was close in every sense of the word."

"I don't want to hear any of your carefree comments. That girl just died, Amanda."

"I'm well aware. I watched it too. Does it really surprise you? I knew something was up."

"How can he control her emotions like that?" Everything is coming together in my mind. This must be why I had been so angry before. This is why I lost control and broke up with Katie. This is why I killed myself. This is why Katie killed herself. It has to be. But why?

"They're angels. They have powers." Amanda shrugs.

"They're not angels. Angels wouldn't kill people like that. So, this place can't be Heaven. You said yourself that you couldn't find someone here that you knew was dead."

Amanda averts her eyes.

"I have an idea." I cross the hall and open the door to the control room. "I have a crazy hunch. You said to remind Katie about me I should show her physical proof and I tried that with our promise rings, but it didn't work. I bet showing her the locket I got her for our third anniversary will wake her up."

"How is a necklace going to be any different than those rings?"

"Because the necklace is still on Earth. It hasn't passed through the gate and become a forgotten memory."

Understanding spreads across her face. "But you don't know how to work those things." She gestures to the basket of golden bracelets.

I take one anyway and glance at some of the buttons Michael had used. Most knobs are labeled with different emotions, but then there is a set of buttons labeled one through twelve. I brush the questions away and focus on the more important task before me. "It's probably easy like everything else is around here. It's all been telepathic. I probably have to think about where I want to go and then poof I'm there."

"Are you sure you even know where this necklace is?"

"It should be at Katie's. I just have to slip in, grab it, and I'll be back here in no time."

"I'm coming with you." She reaches for another bracelet.

I bat her hand away. "No, I need you to stay here. If Michael comes back and we magically appear we're both done for. I need you to stay and make sure I don't get caught coming back."

"You want me to be a distraction?"

"Amanda, we don't have time for this. Yes, I need you to be a distraction. We have to work together if we're going to accomplish anything."

She thinks about my words, then nods. "You're really stepping up, Lover Boy. I'll make sure you don't get caught by Michael." The look in her eyes is sad but she stands confident and ready.

"Thanks. I'll see you when I get back." I think hard about Katie's house and slide on the bracelet. I close my eyes and imagine that I am standing in her bedroom. I can see the rainbow lights she has strung up on her wall and the fluffy pink rabbit I won for her at the fair last year sitting on her bed. I can see her dresser, piled full of books, and a mirror that has photos all around its edges, most of them of her and I.

I open my eyes and what I had imagined is now in front of me. Katie's room looks exactly the same as I remembered it. I shove back the urge to cry. I don't have time to get lost in memories, I have to get back to save her.

I rush to her dresser where her jewelry box is and pull out every drawer. I check them all twice, but her necklace isn't in any of them.

Where could it be?

Suddenly, a sharp pain shoots up my arm starting at my wrist. I look to where the bracelet sits and notice a spike piercing my flesh. Liquid fire alights in my veins and I clench my teeth together to stifle the scream fighting to get out. What the hell? I try to pull the bracelet off, but it doesn't budge, and each pull stimulates the pain more.

I turn my attention back to finding the locket. One problem at a time. I start searching under the books until it hits me. I remember Katie's mom came to my house to tell me the news about her death and she gave me the locket back. My heart was so broken at the time I forgot about it until now.

The necklace is at my house.

I try to think about my room in as much detail as I can, but I don't teleport there. The bracelet must only go back and forth between the Kingdom and Earth. It would take too much time to go back to the Kingdom and then to my room and if Amanda has already distracted Michael once I can't be guaranteed she can do it again without raising suspicion. I'll have to run to my house myself.

I go to Katie's closet and pull out a black hoodie. No one can see my face. There's no way I can explain my way out of this one. I strip the hoodie over my head and creep downstairs. Katie's parents must be asleep. The house is dark and quiet. Anna, Katie's golden retriever, is asleep beside the door waiting for her to come home. "Sorry girl, she isn't ever going to come home," I whisper as I try to open the door quietly.

Anna jolts awake and starts barking loudly. I have to get out of here before I'm caught. I slip out the door and close it. I begin running and when I look back behind me lights are coming on all throughout the house.

I duck down an alleyway and pull the hood over my head. I have the route between our houses memorized so I don't miss a beat and keep running.

It takes only four minutes for me to be standing outside

my door. I pat my pockets. No key. Mom's gardening gloves lay on the bench beside the door. I slip my hand in one and pull out the key we keep hidden there in case one of us gets locked out.

We don't have a dog, so I unlock the door and open it without hesitation. My house is dark and quiet too. I move silently down the hall and into my bedroom. It's just the way I left it; clothes on the floor, paint and brushes strewn all over the desk, pictures of Katie and I taped to the walls. There's just one thing wrong.

Mom is lying on my bed.

I freeze. Has she seen me? I listen closely and her heavy breathing assures me that she's asleep. Why is she sleeping in here? It never really occurred to me until now but since Dad left, I am all Mom has. Until I died that is. Now she's all by herself.

This time I can't stop the tears from coming. I want to run to her side and hold her. I can't even imagine how lonely she must feel.

I don't have time for this.

As painful as it is, I have to stick to the task at hand and that's getting Katie's necklace and returning to Amanda. There's nothing I can do for mom here. I run over to my desk and start sifting through its drawers. Where did I put it? I move everything lying on top of the desk.

You've got to be kidding me.

I look over at my bed. The necklace is hanging on the bedpost next to mom's head. I tiptoe over, thankful I don't have a heartbeat or need to breathe and lift the necklace off the post and stick it in my pants pocket. Mission accomplished.

I look down at mom. Even asleep she looks exhausted. There are bags under her puffy eyes and her black curly hair lays tangled and unbrushed. I wonder to myself just for a moment what would happen if I stayed here. She needs me.

But that's not a possibility. I'm dead. But maybe I can give her a sign that I'm okay. I grab a paintbrush from my desk and dip it in the purple paint, her favorite color. I swipe my brush a few times over the wall near her head leaving an abstract rose. I reach down and very gently touch her cheek. "Everything is going to be okay, Mom. Hang in there. I love you."

I start to think about the Kingdom and Michael's mansion with the small control room. As I feel myself begin to fade, I watch mom's eyes slowly lift open. She looks directly at me. "Scotty?"

But then she's gone.

CHAPTER TWENTY-TWO

Back in the control room I stare blankly at the wall. Mom saw me. Or at least she thinks she saw me. She's probably crying now. My heart breaks at the thought of it. I hope the painting will calm her down.

I look around and whisper, "Amanda?" No answer. I wonder where she is. She probably had to lead Michael away with a silly question. I should get out of here before he gets back.

Walking out the front door of the mansion, I slip my hand into my pocket. It's still there. The cool metal of the necklace makes my hand tingle with excitement. I'm finally going to have my Katie back.

Up ahead I hear voices. Amanda must have lost their attention. I duck behind a tree and listen hard.

"But how did she recover her memories?" That's Matthew's voice.

"I pushed her through the gate same as everyone else. Something is going on and we need her to tell us what so we can put an end to it." That voice belongs to Michael.

I hear the front door to the mansion shut and their voices disappear. They know about Amanda. They've done something with her. They're going to try to make her talk. I don't even want to think about what kind of torture these magical beings are capable of, especially with their ability to manipulate emotions.

And it's my fault. I told Amanda to stay behind and distract them. She was caught while protecting me.

But we both would have been caught had we come back together. After I free Katie, I'm coming back for you, Amanda. I will not let these angels hurt you.

I take off in a sprint. My feet pound on the ground beneath me. If the angels have Amanda, then there's no telling how much time I have. She won't give me up willingly but who knows what they'll do to her.

I push myself harder.

In town, it's quiet and empty. When the people here don't have to sleep anymore, why wouldn't they be as lively as they are in the day? It must just be habit to sleep at night.

My legs begin to ache, but I keep running. I can see Katie's house. I bound up the steps but then stop myself from knocking. I haven't thought about what I'm going to say to her. She told me to leave her alone and to not come back. How am I going to convince her to open the door? She could call angels to come take me away.

I bend over and put my hands on my knees. I'm exhausted from the run and clueless about Katie. And then the idea strikes me. I pull the hood of Katie's jacket that I'm still wearing over my head and tuck my hands into the sleeves.

I walk off the porch back to the path and face the house. I hunch down into a running stance. I'm so done for if this necklace thing doesn't work.

I take off running towards the large window on the side of the house where her living room should be. At the last minute I duck my head and jump, smashing through the glass.

I push myself up off the floor and brush most of the diamond-like shards off. I run to Katie's bedroom and throw open the door. She's huddled on the bed clutching a kitten tightly to her chest. She's physically shaking, startled by the intrusion.

I approach her slowly, one step at a time, and pull back my hood. I keep my voice low and steady. "Katie, I know what you're thinking. I know you're scared but if you give me a minute to explain everything will be okay, alright?"

When she realizes it's me, she becomes angry. "What are you doing here? I told you to leave me alone!"

"I know but listen. I have something that will help you remember. Please just calm down." I'm only a foot away from her bed. I reach my hand into my pocket and pull out the necklace.

"Even if it's possible for me to ever remember you, I hope I never do! You're crazy! And I'll scream if you come near me."

That hurt.

I need to stay calm. If I show I'm not a threat maybe she will relax and trust me. "Katie, let me show you this necklace. If this doesn't work, I will leave you alone, but you have to see that this place is wrong. Do you remember your grandmother? She died. Have you seen her here?"

I don't know if I fully mean it when I say I'll leave her alone because I could never give up on her, but I try to look genuine. She thinks about it and I hold my breath. Hopefully the thought of her grandmother earns me some points.

"You better mean it," she says, and I let the air out I was holding and rush to her side. She flinches at my sudden movement.

"I do mean it, try to focus okay?" I hold the necklace in the palm of my hand in front of her.

"I've never seen this before," she says flatly.

"Please, Katie, try. Look, that's our birthstones. And here on the inside." I open the locket. "See? That's us at senior prom."

She's quiet for a long time. I wonder if the memories are awakening in her. I sit still and stay silent, so I don't distract her.

Finally, she speaks. "Alright, I've given you my time. Now, leave."

I can't believe it. It didn't work. "You didn't feel anything?" I try not to let my voice crack under the heartache. I thought for sure this would work. Amanda's sacrifice was for nothing.

Or was it?

"Put it on." I extend my hand with the necklace still in it toward Katie.

"I did what you asked, and you said you would leave. I'm through with your demands. If you don't leave right now, I am going straight to Michael."

I don't think so. I unclasp the necklace and lunge forward. Her eyes widen with shock. I reach for her neck with the necklace trying not to hurt her by accident. Her hand shoots up to block me, but her fingertips skim the chain of the necklace.

At that moment of contact a bright light blinds me and a force trusts me away from the bed and my back smacks into the wall on the other side of the room.

PART THREE: KATHRYN

CHAPTER TWENTY-THREE

I sit up in my bed and put my hands on my head to stop it from spinning. Disoriented, I look around and try to figure out where I am and what just happened.

I'm sitting on my bed in my new house in the Kingdom. The bright red comforter is balled up at my feet and one of my small black kittens is cowering under it. I pick her up and stroke her silky fur to soothe her.

I glance up when something shiny catches my eye at the end of my bed. I crawl towards it.

It's my locket.

The last few minutes return to me. I remember seeing a bright light and getting knocked backwards after my fingers touched that locket. That locket that Scotty was trying to put on me.

Scotty.

I whip my head around, searching the room until my eyes lock on his body slumped on the floor.

I clamber out of bed as quickly as I can and rush to his side. "Scotty? Can you hear me?" He groans as I lift his head.

"Scotty, please wake up!" A tear slips down my cheek.

Scotty's eyelids lift heavily. He looks at me and lifts his hand to brush the tear that has made its way to my chin away. "Don't cry anymore, Katie."

My heart lifts and I clutch him to me tightly. He makes a painful sound but wraps his arms around me.

"Does this mean you remember?" he asks as I help him stand on his unsteady feet.

I think about it; the blissful three years I have been with Scotty, the chaotic couple of weeks that lead to my death, the peaceful fool I have been living here, and the cowardly jerk I have been to Scotty because of his attempts to remind me. Yes, I do remember it all.

I smile at Scotty. "Can you forgive me for forgetting?"

His eyes light up and he grabs me and holds me as if I might disappear. "It's not your fault. But I'm so glad to have you back." His voice cracks and my heart goes out to him for his persistence against my stubbornness.

"Come, lay down. You hit that wall hard." I lead him to my bed.

"Lay with me?"

"Of course." I shift Scotty onto the mattress and help him lean back against a stack of pillows. Once he's comfortable, he opens his arms to me, and I curl up at his side and lay my head on his chest.

"That's better."

We lay there in silence for a long time, not wanting to ruin the moment with the inevitable conversation of what is really going on around us. Now that Scotty has reawaken the memories inside me, it does make me wonder why they were ever taken to begin with. Scotty sighs deeply and I know he's about to bring us back to face reality.

"This is wrong."

My chest tightens. What's wrong? Us? No, he means the

memory stealing, right? "What do you mean?"

"I mean this place. It's wrong. The Kingdom is not Heaven and those things out there are not angels. They're killing people, Katie."

I have never felt so confused. "Slow down, Scotty, you've lost me."

"It's a bit of a long story."

"That's one cliché I don't like. You have all the time in the world to tell me."

"No, we don't have any time. We have to go and save Amanda. Michael is evil and we have to stop whatever he's doing." Scotty climbs out of bed, straightening his hoodie. Isn't that mine? Or maybe it's one that looks like mine.

My head begins to hurt from trying to keep up. "You need to start at the beginning. I have no idea what you're talking about. And who's Amanda?"

"Amanda is a girl I met here who kept her memories like I did. She has a theory that it's because we refused to pass through the gate. We were pushed through so our willpower made the magic not work, or something like that."

"So how did you bring my memories back? I walked through the gate willingly." I get out of bed and sift through my closet for clothes to replace my fuzzy pajamas.

"Amanda and I followed Michael around at his mansion and these angels can travel back and forth to Earth with these gold bracelets." He flashes the bangle hanging on his wrist. I've seen that bracelet before. I reach for the memory but Scotty continues talking. "When they left, I took one and went to Earth to get your locket. Since it was something that hadn't passed through the gate it was able to let you remember again. I'm still not sure how all this really works."

So that is my jacket? "I'm trying to keep up. What happened to Amanda?"

"She was supposed to stand guard while I was on Earth

and when I got back, she was gone. I overheard Michael say they were going to make her talk." Scotty shifts from one foot to the other and glances toward the living room every few minutes.

My stomach starts to twist in knots. This is a lot to process at once. "Okay, I can buy that this isn't Heaven. This memory suppression is too deceptive for angels, but what do you mean they're killing people?" I pull a white sweater over my head and slide into a pair of blue jeans.

"Everyone is here because they killed themselves," he states, and I involuntarily flinch. "And the angels helped with that. They have this -" A knock at the door stops Scotty from what he was about to say. I look at him as he rakes his hand through his hair and tries to compose himself. "What if it's Michael?"

"He doesn't know either of us have our memories. Let's answer the door together and play it dumb." I reach for his hand. He doesn't hesitate to take it and stands by my side.

We walk to the front door and when I open it, I am met by a face I had pushed away and was glad to briefly forget.

A face with deep green eyes.

Matthew stands on my porch smiling broadly. His body is draped in a long white robe and wings protrude from his back. "Katie, I came to see if you were alright. I see your window is broken. I was also looking for Scott, but it looks like you already found him."

I'm too frozen to speak and Matthew raises one eyebrow.

Scotty squeezes my hand to remind me to play dumb. I blink a few times then force a smile. "Scott's been here hanging out."

Scotty rescues me from blowing our secret by acting flawlessly. "We don't know what happened to the window. We were thinking maybe one of the pets knocked something through it on accident. We plan to get it fixed but right now it's very early and we were still in bed." Scotty hides his wrist with the bracelet still on it behind his back.

Matthew looks at our questionable bedtime attire but seems to accept Scotty's performance and dismisses the broken window. "I also have a few questions for you if you don't mind."

"Ask us anything." Scotty's grip tightens on my hand and I try not to make a face.

Matthew launches into his interrogation. "You've been seen with a girl named Amanda. Do you deny that?"

Scotty feigns puzzlement, furrowing his brow and tilting his head to one side. "Yes, I have spoken with her a few times."

"Did she say anything strange to you?"

"She has a rebellious attitude but other than that no."

"She has broken some rules here and is being dealt with. I was sent to ensure that you were not working with her." Matthew stares hard at Scotty.

Scotty doesn't break composure and I am in awe at his strength. "I didn't know she was breaking rules. What are you going to do with her?"

"That's none of your concern as long as you haven't done anything wrong." His gaze is challenging.

"Of course not."

"Then I'll be on my way. Thank you, Scott." Matthew turns away but then looks right at me and smiles. "I'll see you later, Katie Cat." He winks and walks down the road.

Scotty slams the door and releases my hand to clench his fists. "Can you believe him? It's just sick!"

"Scotty…" The far-off guilty feeling finds its way to me once again.

"Who does he think he is telling me that Amanda is being dealt with and calling you that?"

"He was just trying to get you angry to see if you'd slip

up. But Scotty.." I raise my voice. This isn't going to be easy, but it has to be done.

"What?" I get a glimpse of his anger and it all becomes too much. I drop down to the floor and sobs choke their way out of me. His face softens and he is instantly by my side. "Katie, I'm sorry. What's wrong?" He puts his arm around my shoulder and pulls me in. That's the Scotty I know.

I bury my face into his shoulder and cry until no more tears come. He holds me and waits patiently. Finally, I sit up and look at him. "Scotty, that was Matthew." Of course, Matthew is dead. A part of my living self knew that but never wanted to admit it. But he's an angel?

"I know." Scotty strokes my hair.

"That's the same Matthew that was in my room when you called the night I… killed myself." Speaking of my death makes it feel more real. I really killed myself. The blood in my veins turns cold.

"I've gathered that." His voice comes out strained, but he continues to hold me.

I twist out of his arms and look at him confused. "How do you know that?"

"Just from the things he said when Amanda and I spied on him and Michael."

"Scotty, I kissed him." My voice is barely above a whisper now and I look away ashamed.

"When I was watching them, Matthew put on the bracelet and went to Earth. He pretended to care for a girl who was upset, and she began to feel love for him, but Michael turned a knob that amplified that love and it escalated quickly. Then in the end Matthew really upset her and left. Michael amplified that emotion too and it was so much she killed herself. I'm sure that's exactly what they did to you. The part I can't figure out is why you let him get close to you in the first place."

My chest begins to ache. "He was my friend in middle school. We were close. When he found me at college, I thought it was just luck. I didn't know of his underlined interest in me." Did I have zero say in what happened to me? Or did I let him get too close first? Looking back, all my emotions seem like a blur. I can't tell which were real and which were amplified.

"If he was just a friend to you, then why'd you lie? Why didn't you tell me about him?"

I can hear the pain in his voice and think through my answer. His explanation clarifies so much about my feelings towards Matthew, but even if these angels amplified my emotions, there had to be pre-existing emotions to amplify, right? "I don't know. I guess I was afraid of you becoming angry. Then Matthew kissed me, and I didn't know how to confess to being a cheater."

Scotty hangs his head. "I had been angry a lot in the end. I don't know why I was acting like that, especially towards you."

"Maybe it's the same thing that was wrong with me. I was acting in a way that went against my true self and it was because of the angels. You weren't acting like yourself, so could it also be because of the angels?"

"You have a point, and I've thought that myself. I hope you're right. I was awful to you."

"It's okay, I forgive you." I take his hand in mine and bring it to my lips.

"I forgive you too." Scotty leans in and I soak up the moment he kisses me.

I have missed him deeply, even if I didn't fully know it in my dream state. The countless visions I had of him proves he never left my mind though. I hope his forgiveness is sincere. I don't doubt his love for me, but I know my betrayal, no matter how little I had control over, hurt him. Does he still feel the same for me? Do I feel the same for him after everything? When I finally break the connection, I pull myself to my feet. I hold my hand out to Scotty. "Come on."

He takes it and stands up beside me. "Where are we going?"

"To rescue Amanda, of course."

CHAPTER TWENTY-FOUR

"Whoa, what?" Scotty holds his hands up.

"You said yourself that we have no time to lose because they're probably torturing her, and she helped you bring us back together, so there is no way I'm leaving her in their hands." This new found determination feels good.

"I am going to save her, but there's no way I'm letting you help. I can't risk losing you again."

"Spare me the nobility. You need my help. I'm not losing you now that I have you back either." I begin slipping a pair of flip flops onto my feet.

"I'm not playing this game, Katie."

"And I'm not playing at all. We do this together, Scotty." I watch as he sighs, giving in to me.

"Alright, together." He takes my hand and we walk out the door. "So, what's your plan my brave heroine?"

"You know more than I do about this place and the angels. Where do you think they are keeping her?" We walk hand in hand along the path that leads to town.

"Michael's mansion for sure. It's secluded and seems to

be off limits to us."

"Then that's where we're going. Lead the way."

The town is dotted with a few early risers. Dawn is just below the horizon and the chilly morning air is already beginning to warm. Rich smells of coffees and cakes from some of the shops drift across the breeze to me. If things weren't so serious right now, I would stop in for breakfast.

We bypass the town altogether and crunch on leaves fallen from some of the trees around us. I don't think this place has seasons, but rather a mixture of each swirled together. I allow myself to get lost in my thoughts now that I can think clearly for the first time since I began losing control. Matthew, the guy who I thought was a long-lost friend from my childhood is actually an angel who isn't an angel. He's a killer of so many innocent people, including me.

Was he the only reason I killed myself?

It had to be… Failing grades and lost job aside my life wasn't so horrible that I would end it. My desperate battle for control wasn't a fair one. Sure, I wanted to take hold of my anxiety, but the odds against me were stacked. Without the angel influence I wouldn't have self-harmed or killed myself, right? Losing Scotty was what unraveled it all though. But he wasn't himself for the same reasons I wasn't. I can't hold any of that against him, can I?

Because look at everything he has done to bring my memories back to me. It couldn't have been easy getting my locket.

My locket.

"Scotty?"

"Yeah?" His faraway look comes back to focus on me. He must have been lost in thought too. I wonder if it was about me, or about Amanda.

"I've been wondering, tell me more about how you got my locket?" I stroke the pendent hanging around my neck.

"That's a bit of a long story." He doesn't elaborate immediately, so I wait a few moments to be sure.

"You know I hate that saying," I mumble when he remains silent. He nods. I decide not to push it. He'll talk when he's ready.

The trees begin to break, and a dark structure consumes more of my view as we approach. "This is where Michael lives?"

"Wait until you see inside." He grins, and I shudder involuntarily. Thankfully he doesn't notice, or he would cut me out of this rescue mission completely.

I creep out of the forest and to the front door. Scotty follows closely behind. The door is unlocked and once inside Scotty motions for me to take off my shoes. As he slides out of his I raise one eyebrow at him. Not exactly the right time to be courteous, but he puts one finger to his lips then points at his socks.

Now I get it.

I slide my flip flops off and clutch them in my left hand. Looking in every direction, I don't even know where to begin. Scotty scans the room then starts upstairs. I shrug and follow. I guess he knows what he's doing.

We ascend the staircase on the right since it's closer. None of the stairs squeak and when we reach the landing on the second floor, I let out the breath I had been holding. I'm sure my heartbeat would be echoing in this vast house if I had one. The quiet is unsettling.

We move silently down the hallway past many closed doors lined on both sides. How many are there? Eight? Ten? And is Amanda behind one?

Toward the end of the hall I start to hear a low muffled sound. I put my ear to one of the doors. It sounds like someone ranting. I motion for Scotty and he places his head next to mine. Suddenly a broad smile seizes his face and he quickly reaches for the door knob.

The door doesn't budge.

Scotty jiggles the handle more violently then throws his weight against the door. I put my hands on his chest and push him back, alarm written all over my face. He looks at me then turns away and sighs while running one hand through his ruffled hair.

Finally, he freezes and looks at me, then past me. I turn and follow his gaze. Next to the door is a golden plate with a black number nine. Scotty sets his face then leans very close to my ear and whispers in a voice so low I hold my nonexistent breath to try and be silent enough to hear it. "I think I can get the door open. Wait here." He pulls away and I shake my head. We can't split up, it's too dangerous. He holds up a hand in the 'wait' position. I cross my arms but watch as he glides down the hallway from where we came.

I begin to pace. How long is he going to be gone? How long am I supposed to wait before I suspect something has happened to him? What if something does happen to him? I don't know everything that he has learned about this place.

The questions swim in my head and sweat forms on the back of neck and slips down my spine. My hands feel slick in their clenched fists so I wipe my palms against my blue jeans. I press against the wall and sink to the floor. Can I have a panic attack even though I'm dead? My stomach knots and I curl in on myself. I squeeze my right hand around my left wrist where my cuts are and wince at the pain but press harder.

No. I need to stop this. Isn't this what I was fighting on Earth? For control? The angels aren't controlling me now. I am. Hurting myself isn't the way. It wasn't on Earth, and it isn't here. I'm okay. We'll figure this out. Scotty's fine.

Eventually the tightness in my chest eases and my blurry vision clears. I sit up from the fetal position I had collapsed in. Concentrating on my breathing I manage to get it to return to normal. That's when I hear the sound of the bolt clicking inside the door.

I watch down the stairway for Scotty and within seconds he comes bouncing down the hallway with that same smile from earlier. He grabs the doorknob once more and this time the door flies open from his push.

The room that opens up before us isn't at all what I imagined for a prison. It's well furnished with everything a bedroom needs, including a large canopy bed. Morning sunlight from outside streams in from the barred window casting a glow onto everything it touches, including a short attractive girl standing in the center of the room. She has her arms crossed and a smirk on her face. "It's about damn time, Lover Boy."

CHAPTER TWENTY-FIVE

Scotty rushes into the room and puts his hands on the girl's shoulders. I'm assuming she's Amanda. "Are you alright? Are you hurt?"

Amanda bats his hands away. "I'm fine. Get your paws off me."

I take a moment to look the girl over. She looks to be about sixteen. Her height makes her appear younger but the way she has her brown hair pulled back into a tight bun and the fierce look on her face makes up for it.

She moves her attention from Scotty to me still standing in the doorway. "So, you're Katie? I hope you're worth all the trouble we've been through to wake you up. At least you're cute, I guess."

What am I supposed to say to that? "Thank you?"

Amanda smiles at the disorientation she caused me. "I'm kidding, chill out."

Scotty glances around anxiously. "Amanda, we need to get out of here before the angels come to check up on you." He grabs her hand, but she snatches it away.

"I'm not going anywhere."

"Amanda, we don't have time for this, come on."

"Would you listen?" she demands, and Scotty pauses to look at her carefully. "Michael may be able to manipulate emotions, but I'm not broken so easily. Once he figured that out, he came up with another plan to push me through the gate again. I pretended to be afraid and pleaded for him not to which seemed to please him. If he does it tonight, I'll lose my memories again, but wake up in the morning with them back just like the first time."

"That's too risky. What if they've fixed it?" Scott looks at her hand like he's going to grab it again, but he doesn't.

"First off, they don't even know what the problem is otherwise you'd be in one of these rooms. Secondly, they know nothing about free will, that's why they take it away. Or at least try to. And thirdly, if I did leave with you now, where would we go?"

"But Amanda…"

"No, Scotty. She's right." Both sets of eyes stare at me.

"You know, I'm not sure if you really believe that or if you just want to get out of here." Amanda stares at me skeptically. Truth is, it's a bit of both.

"Amanda! Do not start anything." Scotty walks over to my side. "Katie and I will watch for you at the gate and once you remember again, we'll plan from there."

"Don't talk down to me. I can plan without your help." Amanda turns her back to us. "Now I think you should leave before Michael comes back."

Scotty looks at her for a long moment then turns to walk out the door. I follow, closing the door softly behind me. I reach for Scotty's hand, but it's balled into a fist that won't open for me. "Scotty, it's going to be okay."

"I hate leaving her in there, Katie." His voice is tinged with frustration. "She was caught and put in there because of me. I chose to save you before her. I'd do it that way again, but who knows what they did to her in that time."

"I know." I swallowed my own emotions and hug his rigid body. "We'll fix this, but right now we need to go."

He sighs then nods. We make our way down the stairs of the silent house. At the bottom he leans in and whispers, "Wait here. I need to lock her door back." He starts walking but he's not leaving me this time. I follow and ignore his head shakes.

We reach a metal door down one of the halls and he slides in trying to shut it behind him. What is he hiding? I push the door open and look around. There's a lot of monitors and buttons. Scotty starts pushing a few.

I focus on the screens that feature different people, male and female of different ages, but mostly centered around my age.

"Katie, don't!" Scotty wraps an arm around my waist and pulls me toward the door. When we're out he shuts it but not quick enough to prevent me from seeing the heartbreaking despaired looks on all those faces. On one face in particular. One with wavy blue hair. I don't feel the tears come but by the time Scotty rushes me outside my cheeks are slick with them. He sits me against a tree and falls beside me. Watching me as he slides his shoes on, his eyes say he's choosing his words carefully.

I speak before he does. "What was all that?"

"Do you remember when I told you Michael and Matthew manipulated people's emotions so they would kill themselves?" Scotty pauses to wait for my nod. "Well that's the room they do it in."

"All those people… and Cassie… they're going to die? Scotty, we have to do something! This isn't right!" The sobs threaten to choke me.

"We will. As soon as we have Amanda back this whole thing will come to an end."

I slip my flip flops on and follow Scotty silently back to town. He's so confident in Amanda's ability to bring this system down but why? They just met, didn't they? I push back the small hint of jealousy in my mind. This is ridiculous. I have no reason to doubt him. I'm the cheater, even if I was being controlled.

"I have no idea when they will decide to push Amanda through the gate. If you want to go back to your house now you can, but I'm planning on going there and waiting." Scotty doesn't look at me while he speaks.

I again try to push back the intrusive thoughts of Scotty and Amanda alone together. I know I'm overthinking. He loves me. He's only concerned about his friend. I grab his hand and lace my fingers through his. "I'm waiting with you." I give him a small smile when he finally looks at me.

He doesn't respond but he doesn't let go of my hand either. I begin to wonder how much my betrayal has affected his image of me. I'm sure he needs some time.

We walk back into town. The number of people out and about has greatly increased since early this morning. There's a constant stream of hellos as people greet each other and bells ring above shop doors. Every so often, someone brushes up against me making my anxiety rise. I don't remember there being this many people before. How many of them are new? Instead of going back into the resident side, we make a left onto a small path headed by a sign pointing to the meadow.

It's a short walk lined with blossoming trees filled with songbirds. As soon as the view opens up my eyes sparkle with wonder as they take in the peaceful landscape. It's all as beautiful as the day I first arrived and exactly how I imagined Heaven would look. Maybe when we put things right here, I'll get to go there and live in this perfection forever.

Scotty isn't taking in the scenery as he leads me to a bench on the side of the lake closest to the gate. We take a seat and try to look casual as we begin to wait.

I allow myself to think about Cassie. My chest aches knowing she's being manipulated like I was. She already has self-doubt and fear of being unwanted. If the angels amplified those… I was supposed to call her back. The night I killed myself, she needed me. Did she think I abandoned her?

And Marie, does she blame herself for my death since she left our room when Matthew showed up? And the guys at the shop, do they think if they didn't let me walk home alone things would be different? What about my parents? My death probably crushed them.

How did Scotty take my death? First, he found out I was cheating on him, then I took the easy way out and killed myself. No wonder he's keeping his emotional distance from me. I probably seem psychotic even though it all wasn't my fault.

But I did kill myself, nonetheless. I thought I was taking control of my life, but I couldn't have been more wrong. That moment was a complete loss of control. I let the angels win, but I won't let it happen again I'll save Cassie and all those others targeted by the angels.

After what feels like a couple of hours of dead silence I stand and stretch my stiff body.

"Katie, sit down!" Scotty hisses.

"Scotty, there's no angels around. I'm going to go get a cup of hot tea, would you like one?"

He looks at me exasperated. "What's the point? We don't need to eat or drink anymore. We're dead."

"I want it because it's warm and comforting, unlike how this situation makes me feel. I know you're worried about Amanda, but I also know you're afraid of interaction with me because of what happened with Matthew. I'm trying to bring a piece of familiarity to us so maybe we can reform our relationship. A cup of tea isn't going to ruin our stakeout. "I bite my lip. I don't regret what I said but I'm afraid confronting him will hurt and the angel's anger will slip through.

Instead of a scowl his face softens. "You're right, Katie. I'm sorry. I guess I'm just stressed and worried about saving you and Amanda and everyone else here in this hellhole. I didn't mean to make it feel like I'm pushing you away. Yes, I'd like a cup of tea, four sugars as always."

I nod and head to the café on the other side of the meadow. I know things are tense right now, but I also know things will get better. If we stick together Scotty and I can get through this.

As the person behind the counter hands me my teas, Michael strolls by with his arm around a handcuffed Amanda. Neither of them pay me any mind. I follow behind casually and pick up on their conversation.

"Doesn't it make you look suspicious leading a prisoner around?" Amanda asks in her ever-growing familiar defiant tone.

"In this trance state they're in, they perceive us as nothing more than an angel and human taking a stroll on this beautiful day. The concepts of evil and suspicion don't register in their foggy little minds." Michael shrugs. As we near the gate I veer off toward the bench where Scotty is pretending to be looking out over the water. I hand him his tea and I sip mine in silence while keeping my attention on Amanda and Michael.

"So, you're implying you're evil?" Amanda smiles darkly.

"If that's how you wish to view me then so be it, but as soon as you pass through the gate it won't matter what you're thinking right now." With Michael's words Amanda's smile dissolves into a scowl. I give Scotty a sidelong look. His grip on his cup is white knuckled tight, but he doesn't make a move to take a drink.

"Is that supposed to sound menacing? Anyways you can forget about me passing through the gate because I refuse." Amanda thrusts her chin and delivers a cold glare at Michael. I have to admit, attitude or not, I admire her boldness and bravery to stand her ground in the face of danger.

Michael gives her a dark smile. "Would you like me to take those handcuffs off? I'm sure they're not very comfortable."

Amanda looks momentarily taken aback but then narrows her eyes at Michael. "Uh, sure." She inches toward him and turns her back. I know she has to be pushed through the gate to throw Michael off our trail, but I still have to work hard to suppress the warning for her to run away that's climbing up my throat.

As soon as Michael unlocks the handcuffs, he shoves Amanda through the gate a little more roughly than he needs to. She lands on her hands and knees and an unnatural happy smile spreads across her face.

Michael is quick to help her to her feet. "Are you alright? I know the ride here can be a bit bumpy."

Amanda stands and looks around in a daze. "Where am I? Who are you? What happened?"

Michael holds up a hand to silence her. "My name is Michael, and this is the Kingdom. Your time on Earth has come to a close so this is where you now live."

Amanda looks as if she's thinking about it but then scrunches her eyes shut and puts a hand to her head. "I don't remember dying."

"It was a tragic death, so we have erased the memory to allow you to live peacefully here."

"Oh, okay." She looks around the meadow with wide eyes, taking in the beautiful scenery.

"Now, I have some other duties to attend to, but if you need anything don't hesitate to ask me or any other angel around."

"Thank you." Amanda smiles again as Michael stalks away, no doubt headed back to his mansion to plan the next death.

As soon as he is out of sight, Scotty jumps up, dropping his untouched cup of tea, and rushes over to Amanda's side. I watch the tea darken the dirt, my heart sinks with the liquid.

"Hi, Amanda, I'm Scott." I hear him say as I catch up.

"Uh, hi." She shies away from Scotty. This isn't right. I was just in awe by her bravery and now she's like a scared little girl.

"I want to be your friend. My other friend, Kathryn, and I were getting ready to go to her house for a snack when we saw you arrive. Would you like to join us?"

Friend? I frown at the word choice. Maybe he doesn't want her to feel like a third wheel?

She smiles, warming up to us. "Sure."

We all three begin to walk back to my house. How long will Scotty put this invisible barrier between us? Maybe when we stop the angels and Matthew is no longer around things will be easier. Suddenly, a question pulses through my mind. If the angels caused me to kill myself and that's what they're doing to others, does that mean Scotty killed himself? If so, why? What drove him to do it? Was it my death? Is he someone else I affected so deeply? Maybe we can talk about it later. I can't fix what my death did to those on Earth, but maybe I can fix us.

Once at my door I turn to Amanda. "I should warn you I have quite a few animals."

"Sounds fun!" Her dark almond eyes sparkle.

I open the door and am greeted by a collection of critters. Amanda sits on my couch and plays with one of the dogs while Scotty and I hurry into the kitchen. At some point the angels must have used their magic to fix my window because it's in one piece again and the glass shards are gone.

"How are we going to keep her here until she falls asleep?" Scotty sits at my table, drumming his fingers, while deep in thought.

"I don't know. I could ask her to stay for a sleepover. She seems very compliant in this state. Why does she have to stay anyways?" I don't ask out of anger but rather curiosity.

"We need to start planning as soon as she wakes up, but we can't risk the angels seeing her come here in the morning. That would look suspicious. And I was thinking more along the lines of this." Scotty closes his eyes and furrows his brow in concentration as he conjures the image of what he wants.

Almost instantly there is a knock at the door and Scotty disappears from the kitchen to answer it. When he returns, he is twisting open the newly arrived bottle of sleeping pills. "Pour a glass of milk and get some cookies."

I do as he says, fumbling around in the cabinets for a glass and plate. As soon as I place them on the table, Scotty adds a bunch of crushed up pills to the milk. I know we're dead and can't technically overdose, but does he need to add so many? And why are sleeping pills an option to conjure if we don't have to sleep? Is it just to make the afterlife feel as normal as life?

We walk into the living room and sit the food and drink in front of Amanda. "This looks great!" She dunks a cookie into the milk, eats it, and then chases it down with a long drink. "Your milk tastes a little funny though." After a few more dunks and swallows her eyelids begin to droop, and she begins to sway.

"It'll be alright when you wake up." Scotty smiles and catches her as she slumps over. He lifts her and carries her to my bed.

CHAPTER TWENTY-SIX

Scotty and I stay up all night sitting on my couch in front of the fireplace. The flames cause flickers of orange to bounce on Scotty's skin. Outside, the Kingdom is quiet and dipped in darkness. When you don't have to sleep, why do it? We don't say anything for a long time. It's not an awkward silence but it's not a comfortable one either. Both of us know we have things to say, it's just a matter of knowing how to start that conversation.

As the hours drag by, he begins twisting his ring around his finger, an anxious habit that I've picked up on recently. My animals curl up in their beds, and drift off to sleep, oblivious to anything being wrong. I wonder what life they had on Earth?

Scotty lays his hand on his lap. Without thinking I reach for it, startling him out of his thoughts. His head snaps around to look at me, then at our hands, then back at me. I drop my gaze wondering if I should move my hand.

He hooks one of his fingers under my chin, forcing my eyes to meet his crystal blue ones. "Katie..." His tone implies he has more to say but instead of forming words his lips meet mine. He kisses me softly but behind it there is so much emotion. It's almost like I can feel his heart breaking and mending in a constant cycle. He breaks the kiss and leans his forehead against mine. "I'm so sorry for everything."

I don't know how to respond. Inside, I feel selfish that he's upset because of me but at the same time I'm relieved that at least he's aware of how I'm feeling. I crawl onto his lap and wrap my arms around his neck. This is my Scotty. We're going to be okay.

His arms lock around my waist. I breathe in deep. I've missed feeling like this. I've missed him. The only thing missing is his heartbeat against mine. "It's weird being dead," I mumble against his neck.

"We wouldn't be dead if it wasn't for me."

I shake my head. "It wasn't just you. With losing my scholarships and my job, losing you was too much on top. Plus, you said Matthew was manipulating me and making me feel worse than I should have."

"You lost your job? I'm so sorry, Katie." Scotty moves his head to look at me. "What about the cuts on your arm? I saw them the first day I arrived here."

I freeze. I had almost forgotten about the self-harm hole I had fallen into. How much of my actions were my own and how many were angel induced? Will I ever know?

Scotty must take my silence as embarrassment. He wraps his arms around me tighter. "It's okay, Katie. You don't have to talk about it right now."

I try to believe that all my mistakes are in the past. Dead like us. I crane my neck to give him another kiss, feeling anxious for his closeness. I catch a glance out the window behind him. Dawn pushes the first traces of sunlight over the horizon.

"Ahem." Scotty and I look up to find Amanda leaning

against the door frame from the bedroom with her arms crossed. "Glad to see you guys are having a good time without me."

Scotty quickly slides me off his lap and goes to Amanda. He reaches for her as if to give her a hug, but she steps away from him. "Whoa! Back off! You drugged me!"

"Amanda, calm down. You know I only did that so you would go to sleep and wake up with your memories sooner."

"I couldn't have slept at my house?" Her face flushes red.

"Well..." Scotty looks down at the floor and rubs one hand up and down his other arm nervously. "I wasn't sure if you would actually come back."

"You are so... No, never mind, not the point. Do you really think those things aren't going to come check up on me? If they find me here, they will definitely know something is up with all of us. You clearly didn't think this through, Lover Boy." Amanda starts walking to the door.

"I'm coming with you. If they figure you out, I will not let them take you again." Scotty follows her to the door. I sit quietly and watch, something I do very well.

"If they catch you two at my house it'd be the same deal as here. We'd all be busted."

"Katie is going to stay here and I'll hide if the angels show up at your house."

"We are not splitting up!" I jump up from the couch unable to stay quiet any longer. Both Scotty and Amanda look at me as if they had forgotten I was here. "Amanda, Scotty and I will go with you. We will hide if any angels come but we need to stay together and make a plan. The killing and brainwashing needs to end now."

Scotty doesn't say anything even though he looks like he wants to. Amanda cuts him off before he does. "You know, normally I don't like being told what to do, but your determination is kinda contagious. That, and the fact that you shut Lover Boy up is impressive." Amanda smiles at me and turns back to the door. "Let's get out of here."

She opens the door and cautiously scans the outside. Once she slips out onto the porch we follow closely behind. We file down one street then another, always watching over our shoulders for angels. We don't say anything trying not to bring any attention to ourselves. The day is still early so there's only a couple other people out walking.

We arrive to Amanda's unnoticed. When she opens the door, my head takes a second to wrap around the rustic interior design. I think I feel my jaw literally dropping. Amanda's voice breaks through my wonder." What do you think, Katie?" She stands in the middle of the room and holds both arms out from her sides.

"It's like I stepped from outside into outside. I feel like I'm in the woods. I mean really there." I take a tentative step on the crunchy carpeted floor, marveling at the realism of the sound.

"The outdoors has always been a sort of home to me. If I had a house on Earth, I think this is what it would look like."

Scotty takes a seat on the couch and Amanda sits in a recliner opposite of him. I stand awkwardly until Amanda looks at me again. "What's wrong?"

"Nothing. I mean, well, you two have learned more about the angels and this place when you were trying to wake me up so maybe you'd be better at the planning and I could make some lunch?"

Amanda tilts her head to one side, reminding me of a dog. "You know we don't have to eat right?"

"I know. But doing something normal makes me feel better."

She gives a quirky smile then leans back in her chair. "Well I won't complain, I never say no to food. If you and Lover Boy don't work out, you can move in with me if you're a good cook."

Despite my unease with everything, I catch myself smiling. I walk into the kitchen and begin rummaging through the refrigerator and cabinets for something to fix. I find spaghetti noodles and pasta sauce in the cabinet and garlic bread in the freezer. Sounds good to me even if it is a little early. The concept of time of day doesn't really exist here no matter how hard the angels try to simulate it. Plus, Amanda must like it if it's here.

I dump the sauce into a pot and put it on the stove on low heat then look around for some spices. The spice rack is next to the door leading to the living room. While I pick through them, I listen in to see what Scotty and Amanda have come up with so far.

"Well there's definitely more of us than of the angels from what I can tell, but there's more angels than there are of us who can remember. I don't think we have much of a chance at pulling off anything like a fight because we're outnumbered." Scotty leans forward.

"Okay, how do you propose we wake up more people? Don't tell me you know everyone up here as intimately as you know Katie?"

"Well no, but there has to be a reverse switch to their memories." Scotty sits back again.

I go back to my sauce and stir in some spices. I wonder if we really can wake up everyone else here? No one deserves to have their memories stolen.

I put another pot on the stove full of water to boil for the noodles and lay the garlic bread out on a cookie sheet while the oven preheats. I wonder if there's something about the gate that could bring the memories back? Since passing through the gate causes you to lose your memories, what would happen if you went through it again and your memories were already lost? Do your memories come back? Or do they become double lost? Can you double lose your memories?

I dump the noodles in the boiling water and slide the tray of bread into the oven. Maybe Scotty and Amanda have figured it out by now. I start walking to the living room, but something stops me at the doorway.

Amanda is now sitting on the couch with Scotty. Not closely, but I wonder why she moved. She's looking at her hands while Scotty watches her face. For the first time since I met her, other than after she passed through the gate, she looks like a little kid.

"So, after they died, I was put into a foster home. Between the alcoholic father and the workaholic mother I might as well have lived on my own. Well almost. They had this other boy they adopted, Cory. He was older than me so at first, he thought I was just some stupid kid. I didn't talk to him and he didn't talk to me. But then one day, Mr. father of the year stumbles into my room and starts screaming at me for taking his whiskey."

"Why would he blame you?" Scotty's voice is soft.

"Well I did take it, but he didn't need to yell." Amanda smirks then looks straight ahead unfocused like she's lost in thought. She doesn't move even when she starts talking again. "I told him I didn't have it, but even if I did, he didn't need it. I also told him he was a terrible father and didn't deserve his hardworking wife just to use all her money to live in his drunken stupor. He came into the room and backhanded me so hard I went flying backwards."

"That's abuse! The foster system can't give kids to someone like that!"

"The foster system is a joke!" Amanda whips her head around and glares at Scotty.

I should walk away right now. I should go back to my spaghetti making. I've already heard way more than I was meant to, and it is so wrong to eavesdrop.

166

But Amanda starts speaking again and I can't bring my legs to move. "Anyways, after he hit me, Cory came running in. Apparently, he saw the whole thing and he punched that stupid asshole so hard it knocked him out. We dragged him out to his chair and figured when he woke up, he wouldn't remember anything."

"You mentioned before that you were looking for someone here in the Kingdom and didn't find them and that's how you knew this place was wrong. Who were you looking for? Your parents?" Scotty places his hand on Amanda's shoulder.

"I'm getting there!" She shrugs his hand off. "Cory told me that anyone who can stand up to someone bigger and stronger than them with no fear was alright by him. He and I became real close over the next two years. We took care of each other. We had this little hut that he built out of logs in the woods. He taught me how to hunt and set traps. We didn't need the food or anything it was just fun. A reason to get out of that house and do something. We would spend hours talking. He had a younger sister, Cassidy, who was sent to a different foster home. He always said he would find her one day."

"Did he?"

"You're so impatient."

"I'm sorry."

"No, he didn't find her." Amanda flicks open a pocketknife and shuts it a few times absentmindedly as she talks. "He and I were coming back to the house late one evening. It was getting dark and out Dad comes crashing through the woods with a gun, firing a few shots off into the air, yelling and cussing about his missing alcohol. Cory ran up to him and tried to take the gun away, but it fired, and Cory hit the ground."

"Amanda..."

She ignores him and continues. Every few words her

voice cracks. "I went to his side. His breathing was so shallow, but he looked at me and clutched my hand and said, 'Mandy, you find my sister and take care of her for me. I know she will be safe with you.' I promised him I would, and he smiled but then his arm went limp and I watched the light go out of his eyes.

"I got up and rushed at our Dad, but he brought the butt of the gun forward and knocked me down. He mumbled about how all this was my fault and half carried half dragged me back to the house. He threw me in a closet and locked it. I beat on that door for hours. Finally, police were called when mom got home, and I was taken away."

"Amanda, that's awful. You've been through more terrible things than any one person ever should." He places his hand on hers and this time she allows it to stay.

The timer for the oven goes off and I almost jump through the ceiling. My eyes sting with tears, so I rub my hands over my face and hurry away from the doorway.

I put out spaghetti, sauce, and garlic bread onto two plates and carry them into the living room. Amanda looks up as I approach. Scotty follows her gaze and jerks his hand away from hers when he sees me. I set the plates down on the coffee table and take a seat in the recliner.

"You're not eating, Katie? Spaghetti is one of your favorites," Scotty asks as he twirls a bite of pasta on his fork.

"Oh, I ate some in the kitchen," I lie. But there's no way I could eat after hearing a story like that. My stomach is in knots.

Scotty accepts my answer and begins eating. Amanda plays with her food for a few more minutes but eventually takes a bite. She must like it pretty well because she starts eating faster than she needs to, pushing manners aside.

I've never seen anyone die except in movies, let alone someone that I was close to. I can't imagine what that must have been like...

My thoughts drift back to Mom and Dad again and I wonder how they felt when they learned I killed myself. The guilt sits heavy on my shoulders. How could I have put them through that? And for what? Control? How could I have had it so wrong? I wonder if Anna is still waiting for me to come home. How did Scotty feel? I wonder who came to my funeral? Did Cassie go? Did Marie? Did she have to move out of our dorm room? My mind shoots off into a hundred different directions.

"I've got to say, Katie." Amanda's voice causes my attention to snap back to the present. "I don't really like spaghetti all that much, but this is probably some of the best I've ever had."

"Why would it be in your cabinet if you didn't like it?"

"I ate spaghetti a lot at home. The angels must have noticed that. My brother, Cory, loved it and he was usually the one to cook dinner."

At the mention of Cory's name, I feel the color drain from my face. "Oh Amanda, I'm sorry. I didn't know. If I had I wouldn't have..." A small sob cuts off my words.

"What are you getting so worked up for?" Amanda looks concerned but then realization hits her. "Were you eavesdropping on us?" Amanda stands red faced with her fists clenched.

"I didn't hear the whole story I heard you from the doorway when I was listening to see if you had come up with a plan. I didn't mean to hear what I did."

"I can't believe you!" Amanda raises to her feet.

I should probably be afraid. I don't know this girl, what's she done or capable of. She could punch me right now, and even though I'm dead, it would probably still hurt. But I'm not afraid. I look at her and I see Cassie. I see her lashing out because she's hurting. Losing Cory cut Amanda and I can see her putting on her armor and putting up her wall. But just like with Cassie, I know deep down she just wants love and acceptance.

And also, just like with Cassie, sometimes it has to be tough love.

"Amanda, I was one room over. You know I didn't purposefully lean in and listen to your conversation. You don't need to get so angry with me when there's bigger things going on around us." I keep my voice stern but internally hope she doesn't decide to punch me anyway.

CHAPTER TWENTY-SEVEN

I let out a breath as Amanda backs off. I knew she wasn't as angry as she seemed. She unclenches her fists and her shoulders slump. "Ugh. You're right. Can I have a minute?" Without waiting for my answer, she stalks off to the bathroom. She'll collect herself, then we can stop the angels. All is okay.

I slip out onto the front porch to get some fresh air. I miss Cassie. Helping her felt like having a little sister. She acted out sometimes but once I put whatever the problem was in perspective for her, she always calmed down and apologized. Guiding her helped create a better me, and I'm starting to see that now. Finding my voice and stopping the argument with Amanda was way more control than I thought I had on the bridge the night I killed myself. Part of me wanted to slink away and cry, but that's old Katie.

I sit and lean against the house. There's almost no one outside. They must all be in town. The few people who do pass by don't pay much mind to me. Luckily, I also don't spot any angels. It does seem strange that none have checked on Amanda. Do they trust their gate and magic that much? Or is there something more important holding their attention?

I hear the water splash from the pond beside the house, probably from the ducks playing. A few rabbits scamper by. The door opens and Scotty takes a seat beside me.

For a minute he doesn't say anything, and we let the gentle breeze be the only sound between us. As the time passes, my anxiety returns. We should be doing something.

"You reminded me of how you talk to Cassie sometimes in there," Scotty says, echoing my own previous thoughts.

"I know. She reminds me of her in some ways."

"I saw her at your funeral." Scotty's lips press into a hard line as if he wishes he had cut the words off sooner.

I bite my lip. "How was she?"

"She was taking it hard. I would have believed she'd been okay if I didn't already know the angels were messing with her." He watches me shutter. "Don't worry, Katie. We'll stop them before they get her." He puts a reassuring hand on my shoulder.

"I know. And about stopping the angels, I have an idea about the gate."

"What about it?"

"Well, when I first went into the kitchen you two were talking about trying to get others to regain their memories, so while I was fixing the food, I was trying to think of ways that would be possible. It made me wonder what would happen if someone passed through the gate while their memories were already gone?"

Scotty looks ahead pondering over what I suggested. Seconds later. Amanda busts through the doorway and jumps off the porch. "Let's go, lovebirds!"

Scotty stands up and hops off the porch after her. I stare after them for a few more seconds but then clamber to my feet and trot down the steps to follow. "Where are we going?" I shout trying to catch up.

"You're not the only one who can eavesdrop." Amanda doesn't look at me. "We're going to push some zombies through the gate."

We walk quietly down Amanda's street. When we start nearing town I stop. "Wait, guys."

"What? Want to stop and listen to someone's conversation?" Amanda's comments are snarky, but I can tell she isn't saying them to be hateful. I guess it's her way of trying to brush it off.

"There's always at least one angel in town and in the meadow. I think we should go off in different directions from here and meet at the gate. We won't draw attention that way, especially since they are already suspicious of you two being together."

Amanda studies me, I don't know what she's looking for, but she sighs. "I really hate to admit it but that's probably a good idea. We'll split up and make our way to the gate differently. Stop in a shop or two so you don't look like you're on a mission from God." She smirks.

"Got it." Scotty starts walking off. No see you later or anything?

My shoulders slump but I begin making my own path into the heart of town. I was right about all the people being here. I think there's more here than I've ever seen before. The angels must still be killing. I hope we fix this soon. I scan the faces, hoping not to see Cassie's but knowing if I do, I'd immediately bring her with me.

I slip into the closest shop. Its aisles are filled with candy, chips, and soda. I grab a pack of Skittles and a bottle of Dr Pepper and find an empty booth.

I really don't remember when I started mixing the candy in the drink. Mom always said I was doing it before I was off the bottle. I always laughed and said, "Yeah right." I miss my mom. She's always been there for me. She was my best friend.

It's strange. When I think about the fact that I'm dead I'm sad but not as much as I think I should be. I feel the guilt of hurting my loved ones but it's almost a relief to be away from the stress and the fear in the world. Well, for the most part. Once we put things right here, I think the stress and fear will be gone forever.

I finish off my drink and thank the man behind the counter. I wonder why some people choose to work in these shops. There's no incentive other than the sociability and maybe the feeling of being useful. Maybe it's habit like a lot of things here are laid out to be. Back outside the sun is very warm. I make my way to the meadow.

When I get to the gate, Amanda and Scotty are there and Amanda has a hold of a guy by the back of his shirt collar. "Didn't think you would want to miss this seeing as how you like to know everything." Amanda has no trouble keeping her grip even though the guy is at least a foot taller and has started to struggle.

"Please, let go of me." He twists trying to remove Amanda's hand.

"Okay." She shrugs and shoves him forward and he tumbles through the gate landing on his hands and knees. When he sits up, his expression is blank but then light comes to his eyes and he appears to be recovering his memories.

I go to his side and sit on the ground. "Hey, it's okay. I know things are foggy right now, but it'll become clearer."

He looks at me with big eyes. They're a soft brown, like his messy hair, and framed with bold black glasses. All of a sudden, he starts sobbing hysterically into his hands. I can't make out what he's saying but I rub his back in an attempt to comfort him.

And then, as soon as it happened, he stops. He looks at me with eyes that are less bright and his brow furrows. "What happened?" he asks as he looks around. "How did I get to the meadow? And who are you?"

He begins to stand up, but Amanda puts her hand on his shoulder and pushes him back down to his knees.

"What just happened?" she demands.

"I don't know but I saw it. It worked but only for a few minutes." Scotty runs his hand back through his hair.

"Great. So now what?" Amanda scuffs the ground with her boot in frustration.

I look at the guy on the ground next to me then up at Amanda and Scotty. "What if it's like what happened with you two?"

Scotty doesn't answer but Amanda looks right at me. "What are you talking about?"

"Well you two were pushed through the gate against your will and eventually regained your memories because of it. Then you pushed him," I point to the guy, "against his will and he went back to not remembering."

"So, what do we do? Ask him to go through?"

"That's what Michael did for me. And I didn't regain my memories without help."

"Hey! How about you get up and go through that gate?" Scotty walks up to the guy, his tone soaked in impatience.

"How about you let me go home instead? This doesn't seem right, and I would like to leave." The guy stands up and attempts to walk away but Scotty steps in his way.

"Just do it!"

"I don't want to." The man side steps.

Scotty grabs his arm. "If you don't, so help me, I will -"

"Scotty, stop!" I stand up in front of him and look him in the eyes. "What is wrong with you? This isn't like you. You've been so different for so long. I keep reminding myself that on Earth it was because of the angels but here you're free of that. What has you acting this way?"

I don't wait for an answer and I turn away without looking

at his face again. I walk back to the guy and place my hand lightly on his shoulder. The scene before me echoes a memory of when I was living, and I stopped a bully from harassing a girl I barely knew. " Hey, what's your name?"

"It's David. Can I go home please?"

"David, I'm Kathryn. I know you want to leave but I really need you to walk through this gate. I'll let you go home as soon as you do if that's what you want."

"You promise?" He looks at me and I smile warmly at him.

"Of course. I pinky promise."

He smiles back at me. "Okay." He takes slow steps to the gate. I hold my breath hoping neither Scotty nor Amanda say anything that would make him change his mind.

The moment he steps through, the gate lights up for just a split second but that's all it takes to show me that this has worked. David turns and looks at me. "Kathryn, I have all my old memories."

"I know. That's what we were trying to do."

"But why?"

"The angels here are not real angels. They manipulated you to kill yourself then brought you here and took your memories. My friends and I are trying to get to the bottom of this and put things right."

David puts a hand to his head. "This is all a bit too much. It's like a whirlwind inside my head."

I take his hand and squeeze it. "I know. I felt the same way when they first woke me up." I release his hand and approach Scotty and Amanda. "If we're going to do this, we're going to do it my way. We're not the angels and we're not going to use force like them. These people were used the same way as us and we're not going to treat them like they're any less than us."

Scotty nods. I think he's still speechless over my earlier

outburst. Good, he should be. Maybe we'll get some time soon to talk. Amanda steps forward. "I just have one problem."

"What's that?"

"They're not angels. Can we please find something else to call them?"

"Okay, like what? Are they demons? Fallen angels?"

"I'll think on it. In the meantime, what are we going to do with him?" She tilts her head in David's direction. "We need to wake up more people, but we can't have a crowd forming here."

"Well, you and Scotty are both under watch and I'm probably questionable by this point too, so David? Would you mind if we used your house to keep people?"

"What is your plan when you wake up everyone?" David asks.

I bite my lower lip. "Well... I'm not sure. But that doesn't change the fact that it's the right thing to do to help these people."

"You're right. I'll let people stay at my house. I don't live too far out of town. But if this turns into a fight, I don't want any part of it."

"We're not going to force anyone to do anything."

"Can I go home now before you start gathering people?"

"I promised you could, but maybe you shouldn't go alone, just in case an angel stops you and asks you something." I start walking with David.

"I'm going with you." Amanda speaks up. "Lover Boy, we'll be back. Stay inconspicuous, will you?"

Scotty goes back to the lakeside bench we sat on yesterday. Was that really only yesterday? Amanda, David, and I start walking, choosing to stay on the outskirts of town, dipping behind the buildings, in and out of their shadows. Why did she insist on coming with us? Did she think I was incapable of taking David home myself?

"Where are you from Kathryn?" David sounds like he's trying not to think about everything he just learned. A distraction might settle his mind.

"A small town in West Virginia. How about you?"

"Paris, France."

"Really? That's amazing! But your English is very clear?" I can't even detect much of an accent.

David raises an eyebrow. "No, I'm speaking French like you."

"Oh. It must be an afterlife thing. Everyone hears the language they know."

"I guess I never thought about how that would work. Seems a bit impossible."

"You're dead and living in a world run by angel imposters. How can anything seem impossible anymore?" Amanda shakes her head.

"I suppose you're right." David goes back to being silent as we walk along the road his house is on. A few moments later he stops. "This is me."

We stand in front of an old white farmhouse with a wraparound porch. "You have these in France?" Amanda makes a face. "I thought everyone there lived in fancy houses."

"Well, no and no. I lived in a small house that wasn't fancy at all, but I looked at pictures of houses all the time. I was going to be an architect." He walks up the front steps. "Are you two going to come in?"

"We should get back to Scotty, but we will return soon. Maybe some food and drinks would be nice for the people we bring here to make it feel more comfortable. Can you cook?"

"I should probably just order food." He smiles at me.

I smile back and Amanda and I start walking. I can't hold back the curiosity any longer. "Why did you come with me?"

"Why? Wish I didn't?" Her avoidance of the question isn't

harsh like I expected it to be.

"Please don't ignore the question, Amanda."

She doesn't answer right away, and I begin to think I'll never know why but then she surprises me. "I wanted to talk to you."

My eyebrows raise in surprise. "About what?"

"I shouldn't have snapped at you like I did earlier." Her voice sounds so small. "My past is a touchy subject and I lash out when I'm scared. I also thought that you weren't going to be any help, that you'd just distract Scott and then I'd have to do all this on my own. But then you stood up for David and something about you changed. You just sounded so strong. And back at my house? Well, you sort of reminded me of Cory. He would tell me how it is and make sure my mouth didn't get the better of me."

"I just didn't want to see David or anyone else treated wrong."

"Well I think it's pretty cool of you." She nods her head to herself.

"Thanks Amanda. I promise you I'm here to help. I don't think I could distract Scotty even if I wanted to." I sigh heavily.

"So, the anger outbursts aren't normal?"

"Not at all. He used to be so much more considerate before all this stuff started. The angels made him hateful and in the end that's why I killed myself. You don't think they permanently made him that way, do you?"

"I don't think so. When you were still a zombie, he was a mess trying to wake you up. Between losing you and trying to cope with all of this and seeing his mom again on Earth, he's probably just got a lot going on inside his head."

"When did he see his mom?" Why didn't he say anything about it to me? That's kind of big.

"When he went back to get your locket. Didn't he tell

you?" Amanda looks puzzled.

"No... When did he tell you this?"

"Back at my house when you were fixing food. It's how we got to talking about my parents and Cory."

I stare at my feet. I guess he does have more on his mind than I do. I had no idea.

We make it back to the gate and Scotty rejoins us. "Well, that was quick."

"He wasn't kidding when he said he didn't live far out of town." Amanda looks around. "So, who's first?"

"Let's each find one person. Then I'll take them back to David's. Three doesn't look too suspicious and if we are stopped, we'll say we're going to a house party." I look at Scotty and Amanda for agreement.

"Sounds good." Amanda stalks off looking for someone. Scotty follows.

I head to the cafe where Scotty first talked to me after entering the Kingdom. I want to find the girl who had been my waitress. When I walk through the door, I see her wiping off a table.

"Hello, Belle."

"Oh, hello, Katie. Can I get you something?" She smiles broadly. Her short brown hair frames her face and her hazel eyes shine in the fluorescent lighting.

"Actually, I really need you to come with me for a few minutes."

"Sure. Is everything alright?" She lays down her towel and wipes her hands on her apron.

"Yes. I need your help." We walk back across the meadow to the gate. Scotty and Amanda are both there. Scotty has AJ, the southern girl from the clothing store and Amanda has Jacob, the baker.

"Okay Belle, Jacob, AJ, I need you three to step through this gate please. It would greatly help us out." I smile as genuinely as I can.

They all three look at each other but then tentatively pass through. The same look of awakening that appeared on David's face now consumes theirs and the gate flashes three times.

"They're compliant little things, aren't they?" Amanda speculates.

"I think its deliberate. Another way for the angels to control us." I walk over to our new friends who are blinking rapidly or glancing around as if looking for answers. "I know you're very confused right now and that you have your memories back, but if you come with me everything will be explained."

Jacob begins to pace back and forth while AJ scrunches her eyes together as if trying to understand all this. Belle breaks down and lets heavy sobs climb up her throat. I wrap my arm around her shoulders and lead the group toward David's. The promise of answers keeps them moving. We pass Jeremiah in town. I smile at him and he doesn't stop us. Once past him I let out a sigh of relief.

I knock on David's door and he answers right away. I turn to the small group behind me. "Everyone this is David. David this is Jacob, Belle, and AJ." I gesture to each in turn. "David will explain to you everything he knows. I need you all to stay here and when I bring back more people Scotty, Amanda, and I will tell you all that we know, okay?"

I get some nods and assume that's as much as I'm going to get. I know how much of a shock it is to be awakened. I hope David helps ease some of that for them. I nod at him and walk out the door.

Halfway back to the meadow I see a white cloaked figure walking in my direction. I know it's an angel. I need to stay calm. I drop my head trying to make myself look unimportant as he nears.

Right as he's about to pass a voice that sends chills down my spine addresses me. "Hello, Katie Cat."

Something hard hits the back of my head and I collapse onto the ground. Green eyes fill my blurry vision and then everything goes black.

CHAPTER TWENTY-EIGHT

Beeping. Through the thick cloudiness of my mind, all I hear is beeping. I try to open my eyes, but they are met by a light so intense that its uncomfortable to keep them open. My body feels like it weighs a ton and soon exhaustion sends me back into unconsciousness.

When I wake up for the second time, the beeping is clearer, steadier. I open my sticky eyes and squint in the fluorescent light. I turn my head to the left trying to find the source of the beeping. A row of sophisticated looking machines stare back at me. Their monitors display countless numbers and phrases that don't make any sense.

I turn my head to the right and see a door a few feet away. I try to sit up, but no part of my body responds. I lift my head up as far as I can and see that my body is encased in a round metal shell attached to the hard table I am laying on.

I feel a fluttering in my chest where my heart should be

pounding, and my body begins to tingle. Where am I? What's happening? "Help me!" I try to scream but the sound comes as no more than a whisper. My throat is raw and sore as if I have been screaming for hours.

No one comes through the door. I don't have a very good concept of time, so I don't know how long I lie there. The only thing I can do with this limited mobility is think and study the room. Since I'm not getting anywhere trying to remember what happened, I stare at the ceiling.

It's white tiled. I count 144 tiles. From what I can see the room doesn't look very big. It's a snug fit for my table and the machines. The walls are white too and there are no windows.

I try to study the machines more to figure out what they are. Some have tubes and wires that lead to my metal cast. I'm also pretty sure there are some wires connected to my head. On one monitor I can see my heart rate. All my vitals seem to be monitored. How do I have vitals if I'm dead? On the machine closest to my head, an image of my brain is displayed. What is that monitoring?

The sound of the door unlocking breaks through the now familiar beeping. I turn my head to the right to face my captor.

Matthew strides in, his green eyes scanning the monitors. My heart aches at seeing him again. Was anything on Earth with him real? For me, or for him? When he reaches the table and finally looks down at me and smiles. "Glad to see you're finally awake. I was beginning to miss those beautiful eyes of yours." He slides his index finger over my cheek softly.

I try to move my face away but fail because of my limited mobility. "Let me go, Matthew. This sick obsession you have with me has gone too far. I want to go back to my friends."

His smiles fades, and he turns away from me. "It's not my obsession that I think you should be worrying about. I am merely a small piece in a much bigger game." He turns back to face me. "You, however, are the illusive wild card that we

184

need in order to win."

"I have no idea what you're talking about." This is my best friend standing here in front of me, or who I thought was, but now he's a stranger. The betrayal sinks like a rock in my stomach.

"I know. And as much as I would love to stay and chat, I really should be going." He walks to the door and turns the handle. I can't let him leave. Any information I get from him could help us stop him.

"Wait!" I plead and he pauses to peer at me from over his shoulder. I search my mind for something, anything to say. "Can't I get up and stretch?"

Matthew levels his eyes at me. "Oh, sweet Savior Katie. I can't have you moving around and messing up our progress." He motions to the machines. "They're monitoring your hunger, thirst, and waste levels and maintain your body in perfect stasis. You've been here for two days and I think you're just fine where you are." He opens the door and leaves. I hear the bolt lock into place and then nothing. Just the beeps of my machines.

Two days? I've been here for two days? Where are Scotty and Amanda? Why haven't they tried to save me? Maybe they have. Maybe they've been caught too and are lying on tables in other rooms.

No. I can't think like that. They have to still be free somewhere. But doing what? Do they know where I am? They must be working on a plan to get me out of here. Right?

If Matthew didn't get them, did he get David? Or the others who I brought to David's house?

My head begins to hurt, and my body feels heavy with sleep again. They must have some type of sedative in this body maintaining machine. My eyes start to droop and even though I try to fight it, I feel myself drifting off.

It's easier to wake up this time. The disorientation isn't as consuming. I blink a few times at the annoyingly bright light then turn my neck to relieve some of the stiffness.

When I look to the left, my eyes meet Matthew's. He sits in a chair beside my bed watching me. "Good morning, Kathryn."

I scowl and turn my head the other way.

"Come on, Katie, don't be like that." He reaches over and tucks a piece of hair behind my ear.

"Don't touch me!" I hiss with as much hatred as I can cover the words in. He removes his hand, and we sit in silence for a few minutes. It doesn't look like he plans to leave anytime soon. I roll my head back over to face him. "Why are you just sitting there?"

"I thought you could use the company. You have a visitor coming today and things aren't going to be pleasant for a while."

"Is that threat supposed to scare me?" Because it does but he doesn't need to know that. Who could be coming to see me?

"You know, Katie, I'm not trying to be the bad guy here."

"Really? You destroyed my life, toyed with my emotions, caused me to have feelings for you, led me to my death, and now you're holding me captive on this table hooked up to who knows what. You sure don't look like the good guy, Mattie." I glare at him.

Matthew gives a small smile that doesn't reach his eyes and quickly fades. "You do know that I really am Matthew from your childhood, right?"

"I'd prefer to think you weren't. It's easier that way." I know it's him, but he's changed, and I can't justify what he has done to me based on his adolescent presence in my life.

"I suppose that's fair. After I died, I was one of the first to come here to the Kingdom. Michael took me under his wing, figuratively, and I've been one of his missionaries ever since. I'm not an angel like he is obviously, I just like dressing up and acting the part."

I close my eyes and let out a sigh, feeling my shoulders drop. "You honestly think he is an angel after everything he has done?"

"I see nothing wrong with anything he has done. There is a war coming, Katie. A war between us and the other angels. Michael is following orders to prepare the Kingdom for when they come."

"Following orders from who?"

"Your visitor today. I was told not to ruin the surprise, so you'll have to wait to see who it is." He winks.

I groan in frustration. There're so many things I don't know, and the list keeps on growing. I need to keep him talking though. Maybe he'll slip up and say something useful. "If you are Mattie, then why did you die young?"

"Coerced, like you. But instead of self-harming I got messed up on some drugs. I wouldn't recommend them, Katie, wasn't fun. Dying was the best rehab in existence though. No withdrawal side effects."

I don't reply. I think back to the phone call Mom and I had before I died. She told me about Matthew, but I couldn't believe her. I didn't want to. Can I believe it now? Has he been corrupted by the angels so much that he doesn't know that what he is doing is wrong?

I can't think about that. It's too much and I can't save everyone. I need answers from him, whoever he is. "Why did you manipulate me? Why not Micheal himself? Or another angel? Why is there going to be a war? Who are the other angels?"

"It sounds like you're interrogating me, Katie." He

narrows his eyes at me and smirks.

I stiffen. "Maybe I am."

"Correct me if I'm wrong, but the prisoner generally isn't the one to ask the questions." When I don't reply he sighs. "The angels here can't go to Earth. Which isn't fair since the others can. That's why they enlisted me for the recruitment of humans. And the war started -" The bolt on the door clicks and Matthew turns his head and stands up.

Michael enters the room. Is he my visitor? He looks at Matthew then at me. "Well, Kathryn, you're in for a treat today. Someone is anxious to meet you and really get to know you." His dark smile is sickening and makes me cringe.

"Let's get on with it." The new voice belongs to a man that I didn't notice follow Michael in. He's tall and has long brown hair that reaches his shoulders. He stands out in attire by wearing a black rob and is absent the theatrical wings. Peeking out from his collar are strange scars. They twist up his neck, distorting his skin like burns. His silver eyes look my face over. "Is she ready?"

"Am I ready for what?"

Michael ignores me and studies the machines that I'm hooked up to. "We've brought her immune defenses down but kept her body strong to withstand the procedure. All that's left is adding the final element and manipulating her genetic makeup."

"What?" I try to struggle out of my metal shell knowing that its useless.

"Katie, it's going to be okay. Let them help you." Matthew sits by me and smooths my hair back.

I roll my eyes upwards and clench my jaw in annoyance. Help me? They're not going to help me! I have to find a way to stop them and get out of here! Where's Scotty and Amanda? Why haven't they come for me?

The monitors starts beeping at a rapid pace. I try harder

and harder to move my arms and legs. I won't submit to anything for these angels. Not this time.

"Her heart and brain activity are too high to do this. If we inject her now she'll crash." Michael's silver eyes dart back and forth between monitors.

"Then sedate her!" The man seems to be growing more impatient.

Michael pushes a few buttons on one machine and my body starts to feel heavy again. "I gave her a small dose. Her brain needs to be active. The sedative should keep her still, but she may still be a little mouthy." Michael walks over to the man. "I need you to open your mouth so I can swab your cheek."

The man smiles. "I should say that to a woman sometime. I think it might work in my favor." He opens his mouth and Michael runs a cotton swab around the inside. He then walks back to the machines and puts the cotton swab through an opening of one.

"The machine will extract your DNA, replicate it a few times, and then send it into Kathryn through this IV." Michael picks up one of the tubes connecting me to the machines. "Since her defenses are down her body won't attack the foreign material long enough for me to go in and add it to her own DNA sequence."

"And that will connect her to me?" The man looks skeptical.

"For the type of control you are wanting, I'll need to rewire the brain a bit but yes. Trust me, Cain, I know what I'm doing." Michael pushes a few more buttons and flips a few switches. I try to move but I can't even make my head turn. My mouth feels too sluggish to make words to protest or to beg or anything.

I'm helpless.

I feel something slowly seep into my body. It feels like

fire. It spreads through every inch of me. I can't see what Michael is doing but he's at the machine that is hooked up to my head.

Suddenly my brain feels like a boiling pot of hot water. Everything burns. My lungs force up enough air for a shrill scream to drag itself out of me. My vision goes dark from the pain. I feel myself losing consciousness. And then everything's gone.

CHAPTER TWENTY-NINE

Wake up.

The voice sounds so distant yet so close. I struggle to fight through the curtain of sleep. My hand reaches up and wipes my damp face. Is that tears or sweat? My body shivers and my puffy eyes pry open.

I reach down and throw the heavy blanket off my body and grimace at the hospital gown that covers me. Then it strikes me, I'm free! No metal shell, or tubes, or wires. I jump up on my feet but instantly collapse to the floor. My body is stiff from laying still for so long.

My hand finds the chair next to my bed and I push myself back up onto my feet. I stretch and feel the tension release in my legs, my back, and my arms.

On the chair I notice a pile of folded clothes. They're plain and not what I was wearing when Matthew took me, but they're in my size and more practical to wear to escape in than this flimsy paper gown. I pull on the white undergarments, black T-shirt, and jeans and at the bottom of the pile there's a rainbow belt. Matthew's touch? There's no shoes. I look around. Where do I go? Won't they just find me again? And why did they free me from my restraints and leave me clothes?

Go out the door.

There's that voice again. Its inside my head and it's my voice but it sounds so foreign, like it doesn't belong there.

I shake my head. It's probably the medicine wearing off. I make my way across the room and open the door, shocked that its unlocked. Peering out into the dark hallway I don't see or hear anyone.

Go left.

My instincts must be kicking in. I don't remember being brought in here but maybe I was awake enough for my subconscious to secure the memory. I turn left and tiptoe through the darkness. Is it nighttime or is the mansion always this dark? The black floor and walls are a big change in scenery from my white prison room.

Stop.

My feet stop moving. I frown, puzzled. I didn't have any intention to stop. What is going on?

Open the door on your right.

I reach for the doorknob. This quick response time in communication between my brain and my body is dizzying. The door swings open and inside there is a round black table like in a conference room. Seated at the table is Michael, Matthew, and the guy I just met. Was his name Cain? Why did I come to this room? I'm already caught before I've even tried to escape.

"Well Kathryn, how are you feeling?" Michael sneers at me. I stare, unable to form words.

"Wait. Something doesn't seem right." Cain frowns and his brow creases as he thinks.

Bow.

Bow? Why would I bow? Why would I think that? Regardless, I bend forward awkwardly to the three captors, and torturers, staring at me. Something's wrong with me.

"That's better." Cain leans back in his chair and Michael laughs. The sound makes my stomach clench. Why are they so relaxed? I'm out roaming the halls and they don't seem to care. "Kathryn, I believe Michael asked you a question."

Answer him.

I search for words, but they tumble out of my mouth without much assistance. "I'm feeling okay now that I'm up and moving again but my head seems to literally have a mind of its own." Why did I tell them that? Maybe they can tell me what's wrong since they were the ones pumping meds and who knows what else into me.

Cain looks at Michael skeptically.

"It's a new normal that she will get used to. She can sense it, maybe even question it at times, but since it's tapped into her own brain, she can't do anything about it." Michael says to Cain as if he's trying to reassure him of something. "I also erased the memory of the conversation we had in front of her so she wouldn't know exactly what we did."

"Does this control have limitations?" Cain asks Michael. They both ignore me, but Matthew watches my face with a look of wonder.

"None. She will do anything."

"Even if she knows?" Cain gives me a sidelong glance. Even if I know what? What are they talking about? What did they do to me?

"It doesn't matter. Your will is there and she is not strong enough to break it."

"Even so, just to be safe." Cain looks directly at me.

Don't think about this conversation.

What conversation? I shake my head again. Why is Matthew watching me like that?

"Why not test her? See what you can do?" Michael asks. "Think of something simple that you don't believe she would do on her own."

Cain looks as if he is in deep thought then comes back to focus on me. "What is your opinion of Matthew?"

Answer honestly.

The words that come to mind I couldn't have picked better myself, even though I did pick them, right? "I used to like him a lot. Even when we were kids, I had a crush on him. After he moved away, I always wished he'd find me again and then it would be like one of those romance movies and we would fall in love. Between that delusion and Michael's emotion manipulation, I developed feelings for him. Now that I am here, and I see him for what he truly is I feel betrayed by him." Why did I tell him that?

Cain's eyebrows raise. "So, you would say you hate him now and all those previous romantic feelings are gone?"

"Yes."

Kiss Matthew.

Why the hell would I kiss Matthew? I just said I hated him. What is going on? What is wrong with me?

Even with my panic rising I walk around the table to where Matthew is sitting. He looks up at me in confusion. I lean down, putting my hands on his face, and bring my lips to his. Kissing Matthew now is like a stab to the heart. I do feel betrayed by him, but I don't think it's all his fault. And even worse here I am, yet again, doing this behind Scotty's back.

Matthew kisses me back, his lips mold to mine, but he is the one to break away first. He turns his face from me. "Was that necessary Cain? I think that was torture for both of us."

Cain's smile is dark. "Do you hate her too?"

"No. It was torture because I knew it wasn't real."

"It was never real. Get over it." He waves a dismissive hand.

I don't understand. It seems that somehow Cain knows what I'm doing when I don't. He did something to me, but what? Can he read my mind?

"Kathryn, why don't you take a seat while we finish talking?" Cain gives me a glance. I sit hoping they will say something I can use later to bring them down with Scotty and Amanda when I make it back to them. And I will make it back to them. I promise that to myself right now. Pinky promise.

Nothing in this conversation is about you.

How could I know that? Somehow, I do. But whoever it is about they must be important, and I need to pay attention to every detail I can.

"I am impressed with your work Michael, but I am questioning yours, Matthew." Cain stares at Matthew so intensely that I feel like he's going to catch fire any minute.

"You told me to find someone who could multiply and lead your army and that's what I did." Matthew leans back and kicks his feet up on the table.

"I told you to bring me the best. What you have brought me is a lamb to lead sheep against wolves."

"What I brought you is an alpha wolf disguised as a lamb."

"Explain yourself." Cain drums his fingers on the table.

"Well first off, she is a part of the group that have regained their memories and not only that, but she helped bring back the memories of four others as well."

Cain's fingers stop and his body goes rigid. "How?"

"She used the gate! Cain, I'm telling you she's clever." Matthew sits up and slams his fist down onto the table. "She may be shy and quiet but she's observant and she has a charismatic quality about her. All she has to do is smile and ask nicely and people do whatever she wants. It's not just here in your Kingdom of mindless sheep either. I've seen her do it on Earth. If you just turn up the charisma dial, she will be beyond persuasive. You'll have all of humanity at your fingertips." Matthew smiles pleased with himself.

I have no idea who they're talking about, but she sounds incredible. Incredible and dangerous.

"And you think she's capable of handling this?"

"She has determination like no one I've seen before. If it's in her head to do something, then she will do it. And if you're what's in her head, well then, you can see the potential I'm sure."

"Very well. Matthew, we'll try out your choice in the upcoming battle that I sense is coming. We'll see how strong your lamb is." Cain turns back to me. "Can we talk privately, Kathryn?"

"Uh, sure." What would he want to talk about with me? Maybe he thinks I know who he and Matthew were talking about, but I don't. There must be another group of people who have regained their memories because I know it's not me and it can't be Amanda. She's anything but shy and quiet.

Michael and Matthew stand up and leave. As the door closes behind them, I almost wish they had stayed. Cain creeps me out.

Answer all questions put to you by Cain.

Well I don't think I had much of a choice anyways. If I refuse Cain, I feel like he could snap his fingers and I'd cease to exist. Is that possible?

"We will start out easy. How did you die, Kathryn?" Cain studies me like I am a science project. That's starting out easy? What else is he planning on asking?

"I killed myself by jumping off a bridge."

"When you entered the Kingdom did you keep your memories?"

"No, when I passed through the gate for Michael, I lost them, but then Scotty brought them back." Why did I tell him that?

"How did he do that?"

"He went back to Earth and got a locket that he had given

196

me and somehow it woke me up." Shut up! Shut up! Why can't I stop? He's going to go after Scotty because of this!

"How did he go to Earth?"

"He used a gold bracelet he found here." It's like I don't have control over my own mind. But if I don't… who does? Or how? Or why?

Cain's eyes alight at the mention of the bracelet and his smile grows dark in contrast. "How did he keep his memories when he entered the Kingdom?"

"He and Amanda said it was something about free will. They were pushed through the gate and their memories came back on their own."

"How did you get the memories back of the other four?"

"I asked them to go through the gate a second time." Cain is learning too much. Why am I telling him all this?

Cain sits quietly in thought. That round of questioning must be over. What else is left for him to ask? I should take this chance to question him. "Who are you?"

"Did I say you could speak yet?" His anger flares up.

I know I should stay quiet, but I answer anyway. "No."

The anger fades as quickly as it came, and he looks at me in amusement. "How much do you know about Adam and Eve's first two children?"

"Their names were Cain and Abel. Abel was a good, hardworking person and won favor with God. Cain became jealous so he killed Abel."

Cain smiles but there is no humor in his eyes. Is he really that Cain? The one who murdered his own brother when the world was beginning?

"What is it that you and your friends are planning?" he asks. I guess he found more questions.

"We want to give everyone back their memories and then somehow stop you and your angels." That, at least, felt good to say.

He brings his fist down onto the table. "That is not going to happen!"

Leave. Go back to your room.

Is he going to let me leave if I try? I stand up and watch him cautiously as I head for the door. Once in the hall I retrace my steps back to the room I woke up in earlier.

What do I do now? I look around the room. My eyes stop at the door. Why don't I run away now? No one is watching.

I take quick steps to the door. This is going to be easier than I thought. I grab the doorknob, but it starts to turn in my hand and the door opens with Matthew standing there holding a tray of food.

"Where do you think you're going, Katie Cat?" He kicks the door shut and walks over to the bed to sit the tray down.

"Don't call me that."

"Hey, I'm not the one who kissed you." He holds his hands up in a gesture of surrender. Then he laughs as if this whole thing is a game. It probably is to him.

"I only did that to look weak so maybe I'd get the chance to escape but no, I get you." That was the weakest lie I've ever told, and he knows it. Why did I kiss him?

Matthew puts a hand on his chest. "I'm hurt. I thought you'd be happy it was me and not Michael bringing you dinner."

Secretly I am glad its him, but I won't admit that to him. "It's not like I have to eat anyways, so you can take that food away and leave." I turn my back to him and cross my arms. Then I let them relax. "But you said the machines were monitoring my hunger…" My words trail off as I start to question that. How did I have hunger? And vitals? And my heartrate went crazy…

"It was. In order to do what Michael had to do he had to temporarily bring you back to life. So technically you probably were famished."

I whip around to face him. "I was alive?"

"Only for a few hours. No big deal." He gives a dismissive wave.

"If you're going to keep making words make them good ones." No big deal? I was alive!

"Fine, what words should I say?" Matthew hops up on the bed and swings his legs while watching me.

"What are you?"

"A dead man." He chuckles.

"But your eyes turn silver?"

"I have angel blood in me so I can act as a transmitter when I go to Earth and Michael manipulates human emotions." He nibbles at one of the sandwiches from the tray.

"How does the transmitting thing work?"

"It's really my emotions that Michael controls from the monitors, but instead of me feeling them I can push them onto someone else. I just have to be in the vicinity and you basically become my empath on a more extreme level. It also works better through touch. That's why I'd play with your hair or hold your waist. Well, one of the reasons. It also works better on people who are already emotionally unstable. That's why everyone here is similar in age, because being a young adult is so hard." He lets the sarcasm in on the last part.

He's actually going to answer my questions? I need to learn all that I can. "What is Cain?"

"Same as me but more powerful. He's our leader."

"What is Michael?"

"An angel." He rolls his eyes and looks at me as if that one was obvious.

"He's not an angel. What did he do to me? Am I going to be like you?"

"Not exactly. You don't have any angel blood in you."

"Then what am I?" Are my eyes silver now?

"I can't tell you that. You're just something different."

"Of course not." Frustrated I start to walk the length of the room. Once I reach the wall I stop. "You were going to tell me about a war earlier. Tell me now."

Go to sleep.

Why would I want to go to sleep? Even though I'm against the idea, I still feel the heaviness pull against my body. "Get off my bed, I want to go to sleep."

Matthew moves and pulls back the blanket for me. "Yeah I didn't think he'd let you go much longer," he says quietly as if to himself.

"Huh?"

"Nothing. Sleep well." He walks over and opens the door as he flips off the lights but then turns back to me. I watch his dark figure framed by the light from the hallway. "And, Katie? Even if you do escape from here, you will never be free of Cain." His voice is low and sad. Not threatening. He closes the door and the last thing I hear is the bolt clicking in place.

CHAPTER THIRTY

Wake up.

My eyes fly open. How long was I asleep for? I don't remember falling asleep. I sit up and stretch. Only moments pass before I hear the bolt in the door open. I'm not surprised to see Matthew waltz in.

"Are Cain and Michael too high and mighty to be on prison duty?"

"I volunteer to be the one to check up on you." Matthew strides across the room and sits in the chair.

"Why?"

"Well for one, you're probably lonely and those two won't talk to you unless it's to get more information and two, I just want to see you."

I think about that for a minute. He sounds so sincere but how can I trust anything he says? "What do you guys have planned for me today?"

"Something that you will like at first but only because you don't know what's really happening."

"Could you be any more cryptic?"

"I could actually." He cocks his head to the side.

"Figures." We sit quietly for a while. "How long do I have before I find out?"

He shrugs. "I'm not sure but it's not right now."

"You say so many words without really saying anything." I shake my head.

"Well, it's not my call."

"Then if I have time, can you tell me about the war now?"

"You're just dying to hear that story, aren't you?"

"Yeah, so much so that I'm already dead." A small smile plays on my lips while Matthew freely laughs out loud.

I lay back down, roll over to face Matthew, and prop my head up on my hand. Matthew leans back and begins talking. "The war started back in the beginning after some angels descended into Hell. Even though they had their own place they still thought that how the other angels lived was better. It wasn't jealousy exactly, they just wanted to be equal."

"Why did they leave to begin with?"

"Different views about humans. The angels that stayed in Heaven wanted to leave the humans be after they died. The angels from Hell thought that was wasteful. They thought the humans could be used for other purposes."

"Like being soldiers in their army?"

"That wasn't the plan to begin with. They thought about populating other planets and giving them another life. Using them as soldiers is only a necessity now."

"If Cain is your leader does that make him Satan? And where is God? He wouldn't allow all this killing."

"God and Satan are more like ideas that people have personified, not actual beings. They have a mental presence in the minds that accept them. They can tell the angels what to do and give them the power to do it, but that's about it."

I ponder that for a moment. I see how that can still fit religious beliefs but it's still a crazy idea. "Since Cain is your leader then who is the leader of the angels in Heaven?"

"Who do you think?"

"Abel?"

"Ding ding! We have a winner!" He waves around jazz hands and I roll my eyes and catch myself smiling again. I hide it before Matthew continues. "Cain is convinced that Abel has an army of humans himself and is going to lead an attack here on the Kingdom any day. That is why we have been gaining so many humans lately. Cain wants to be ready to protect the Kingdom and his angels."

"If Abel didn't want to use the humans to begin with why does Cain think he is going to now?"

"Because Abel is a backstabber and a liar." Matthew's fists clench.

"Did Cain tell you that?"

"Yes, but it's true, Katie. I can feel it."

"Probably because you're laced with their blood."

Matthew doesn't respond.

I begin to fear that I've upset him too much and that he's going to leave so I change the subject. "When we all died why did we come here? I know I'm not perfect, but I thought I'd go to Heaven."

You didn't die when you were supposed to. We sort of rerouted your death and therefore your destination."

"Where is the destination exactly? Is the Kingdom a part of Hell?"

"We're outside of Hell but it still belongs to Cain. He created this replica of Heaven for his followers to live in so Hell itself could be used as a punishment place for bad people. Cain has chosen to share this place with the humans he has gained from Earth."

"It's so strange."

"What is?"

"The way you call Michael and the others angels. They're

essentially our idea of demons, but they're not at all what I imagined demons would look like."

"What did you expect? Did you think moving from Heaven to Hell would automatically make them ugly and grow horns? They're angels, Katie. They just live in a different place and have different ideas."

"I'm still not convinced that they aren't evil. I think a part of you knows it too, Mattie, but you're too afraid to admit it. My friends and I will stop them and set things right. Maybe then you'll see who's side you should be on."

Matthew's eyes grow cold. "Have you stopped to think why your dear Scott is still acting like a jerk? You might think you have this all worked out with your friends but remember who's in charge here. Just because he's dead doesn't mean I can't still mess with his emotions. I do enjoy playing matchmaker."

Anger starts at my core as a slow burn, then ripples through my body filling every extremity with heat. "Leave him alone! Leave all of us alone and go to hell!" I turn away from him and glare at the wall. How could he make me question Scotty all this time? I knew there was something up.

Matthew sighs and stands up. "I think you're the one who is going to start seeing things differently." He walks across the room and out the door. I listen for the sound of the bolt, but it doesn't come. I sit quietly and wait for someone else to enter but no one does. Did Matthew give me the chance to escape?

Don't leave yet.

I shouldn't leave. If I'm caught, I don't even want to think about what kind of torture I'll be put through.

There're so many thoughts in my head. Angels from Heaven, angels from Hell, Cain, Abel, it's so much to take in. Hopefully I can remember it all when I see Scotty and Amanda. This information could help us.

My biggest question now is why does Cain think Abel is

leading an army here against him? To stop him from killing the humans? But isn't Cain only taking humans to combat Abel? Who's right and who's wrong?

I hadn't noticed at first but I'm pacing the room. My feet stop when I hear the door creek open. I turn to face it. It must be time for my surprise. Standing in front of me is a surprise but not one I was expecting.

Scotty and Amanda enter the room. We all three stare at each other for a moment, unbelieving. Then Scotty rushes over and throws his arms around me. "Katie! You're alright! We've been searching rooms for you! Please tell me you still remember us?" He pulls back to look at me and puts his hands on my face.

"Yes, I remember you. They didn't take my memories. I'm so happy to see you!" I lean forward and kiss him, relieved that I'm finally getting out of this place. He kisses me back and I feel that this is the Scotty that's been here the whole time, not the one Matthew has been manipulating to toy with me.

"Come on guys, you can make out later. We need to leave now." Amanda leans her head out into the hallway, scanning for any threat, then motions for us to go through. Scotty takes my hand and we leave the room. Amanda falls in behind me and puts a hand on my shoulder. "Glad you're okay."

"Thanks." I say as we start down the hallway.

Take them out the back door. Turn around.

I should be able to find the back way, and it sounds safer than walking out the front. Hopefully Scotty and Amanda will trust me. "Guys let's go out the back way, follow me." I keep a hold of Scotty's hand and turn to go the other way.

"Wait. This way is quicker, and it's the way Lover Boy and I came in. It's all clear."

My head starts to pound as the anxiety grows in me. I have to find a way to convince them.

Lie.

If I can come up with something, they might believe me and follow without question. "I don't want to go back down that hall. I can't. Too many bad things happened." It's not a total lie at least.

Scotty looks at me with concern filled eyes. Amanda sighs and gives in. "Okay, lead the way."

But I don't know which way to go. I creep down the hallway until it opens up. There's three ways we could go, and the angels could be anywhere. Why did I insist on going this way?

Make a right. The back door will be at the end of the hall.

I didn't realize we were that close. That must be why my brain told me to go this way. I motion for Scotty and Amanda to follow and we quickly reach the door that will lead us to freedom.

The late evening sun feels refreshing when it hits my face. I was locked in that room with no windows for too long.

We make our way into the forest and when it seems like no one is following us the tension eases. Finally, I can't hold it in any longer. "What took you guys so long? I was there for at least two days. What have you been doing?" The tears threaten to come but I can't cry now.

No one answers at first, but then Amanda speaks up, avoiding the question. "It's been over three days."

Has it really been that long? I spent so much time asleep it's all a blur. I look at Scotty with questions pouring out of my eyes. Finally, he sighs. "We were told not to go after you because of fear that they were going to turn you into a weapon to be used against us."

That hurt. Am I not worth that risk? "Who told you that?"

"The real Michael."

"The real Michael? I don't understand."

"I'll explain what I know on the way. Then, when we get

back to David's house, Michael can explain the rest."

I nod slowly. The real Michael. Does that mean the angels from Heaven are here? Or is this one of Cain's tricks?

"When you didn't come back to the gate, we didn't think much about it. We thought that you were more comfortable at David's or that you were helping to calm everyone down. So, we continued to gather people and have them pass through the gate. When we had six more, we were starting to head back to David's but then the gate started flashing and everything got bright. When it all faded there was an angel standing there and I thought we were busted for sure. He told us his name was Michael and that we shouldn't be afraid."

"How can you so easily trust him though after you've seen what this Michael has done?"

"We can't, but he answered our questions and told us things the other angels wouldn't want us to know. He also didn't try to take our memories away which is a bit of a big deal here."

"I guess you're right." I still feel skeptical.

"We took him to David's and showed him what we had been working toward. That's when we found out you weren't there. I knew there was something wrong. Amanda and I were ready to go get you right then, but Michael warned us that it was probably a trap."

"But you did come after me. What changed his mind?"

"He doesn't know we went after you." Amanda chimes in.

"What? What's he going to do to me when I show up?" I start to feel scared, panicked even.

Scotty stops to face me and takes my hands. "Katie, you have nothing to be afraid of. I'm positive Michael is a good angel. As soon as he talks to you, he'll see you're not a threat."

I focus on slowing my breathing back down to normal. I shouldn't have anything to worry about. I'm not a weapon. I am away from Cain and whatever he was doing to me in the conference room.

We start walking again. I can see David's house from here and I feel my nerves rising inside of me with each step despite the reassurance I just had. Everything's going to be okay, I keep repeating to myself. A man in an angel's cloak stands outside the door. He has black hair and light grey eyes, a striking combination. There's stubble on his chin and jawline. He's tall and has broad shoulders, nothing like the Michael who is sided with Cain. His wings are folded down making him appear less intimidating and more approachable.

When we stand before him, he lowers his gaze and makes eye contact with each of us. I avert my gaze quickly. When he speaks his voice is soft but full of authority. "Scott, I thought I was clear when I said it was too dangerous to go after Kathryn until we knew what was happening."

"You were. But I thought I was clear when I said I loved her and couldn't leave her there alone. She's the same old Katie. Talk to her and you'll see they didn't turn her into anything evil." Scotty, who is standing in front of me, blocking most of Michael's view, steps aside.

Michael's eyes look me over, not in a checking me out sort of way, but I still feel self-conscious. His gaze stops at my face where he holds my eyes in his. "How do you feel, Kathryn?"

"Physically I feel okay, but I'm really confused as to what's going on and who you are or how you got here."

He nods. "Let's go inside and maybe I can clear some things up." We all file in through the door. The living room is full of chattering people. Michael weaves us through and we make our way to an empty back room. Sitting cross legged on the floor Michael begins. "I am the true archangel Michael from Heaven. The angel here pretending to be me is Samael. He followed Cain when he chose to form Hell."

"So, Hell wasn't formed until after Cain died? When I was

held captive by Cain, I learned that Satan and God are ideas not real beings. Is that true?"

"There wasn't a need for Heaven or Hell until there were humans to separate the ideas of the two sides. And calling God and Satan only ideas drastically downplays their presence. They are ever flowing telepathic beings always speaking in my ears. Just because they don't have a physical form doesn't mean they're not powerful."

"Why have you allowed Cain to take all these people? And what is the war between the angels from Heaven and the angels from Hell really about?"

"For a prisoner you learned a lot." Michael raises an eyebrow.

I blush and avert my gaze. "I sorta made a friend."

"Well I hope that we can free your friend when this is all over. Since the angels that followed Cain were the same as those of us who chose to stay with Abel, our power is matched. Abel and I made it impossible for Cain's angels to step foot onto Earth so they couldn't corrupt the humans. It seems they have found a way around that and Cain had Samael create a shield around this place which he calls the Kingdom so we could not get passed it to stop him from killing innocent humans. That is, not until you weakened it by using the gate in reverse. That is how I was able to get through."

"And the war?"

"Cain convinced the angels that followed him that they were superior to humans and deserved to live in luxury with humans as their slaves. We who followed Abel, of course, didn't agree and told Cain he would have to leave Heaven. We gave him Hell and the authority to rule over those humans who couldn't be allowed to enter Heaven due to their actions of Earth. They turned part of Hell into a replica of Heaven for themselves. That's where we are now."

"Where's Abel now?"

"He's waiting just outside the Kingdom for when the nearing battle begins. We need to end this and take away what power Cain and his angels have."

"I agree. How can I help?"

"Anything you learned when you were held prisoner could greatly help."

Lie.

"I didn't learn anything other than what I told you."

"That was more than I expected. Let's hope we can use it to our advantage."

There must be something else I can tell Michael. I scrunch my eyebrows together and try to think through the confusion. Just then David pokes his head in. "I'm sorry to interrupt but there's an angel out here saying he needs to talk to Katie. I don't think he's on our side, but he says he's not leaving until Katie comes out."

All eyes in the room fall on me. I stand slowly. It's hard to move because every bone and muscle in my body is trembling. It has to be one of Cain's angels. None of Abel's know me. Am I going to be taken away again?

Step by step I walk back to the living room. The buzz of conversation has dulled to whispers. I look around the room at the people sitting in chairs and on the floor all of whom are looking back at me. Then some turn their heads and I follow their gaze.

Matthew stands in the doorway, dressed in white and frowning with a darkness shadowing his green eyes. "We need to talk, Katie Cat."

CHAPTER THIRTY-ONE

I walk to Matthew. Despite everything I am not afraid of him, but still angry. "Okay Mattie, let's talk."

His eyes dart around to meet all the stares he is receiving. "I'd feel better if we did this outside." He leads me out onto the porch. As the door is about to shut a hand catches it. Matthew glances up. "I'd prefer this to be private Scott."

I turn to look at Scotty and Amanda who have followed me outside. Michael tentatively stands in the doorway halfway concealed by the door.

"There's no chance we're letting her out of our sight with you. Why don't you just get out of here?" Scotty's words are dipped in hatred.

"Look, I'm only here to tell you that Cain and his angels are coming." Matthew puts his hands up.

"What? You're warning us out of the kindness of your heart?" Amanda scowls.

"I just care about Katie, okay? I thought she deserved to have a heads up before Cain dealt his wild card. If you want someone to blame for all this, you might want to turn around."

Matthew nods his head toward Michael who lifts his chin as if to accept the challenge.

The tension grows thicker when Scotty takes a few steps closer to Matthew. "You care about Katie? What the hell are you playing? You're the one who kidnapped her! You're the one who made her kill herself in the first place!" Scotty's glare hardens his entire face.

I take a deep breath and step forward until Matthew and I are only inches apart. I can feel Scotty and Amanda ready to pounce behind me and I'm sure this situation hasn't made Michael too comfortable either, but I reach my hand out and touch Matthew's arm. He looks at my hand then back at my face. I try to look as open and sincere as possible. "Mattie, everything Cain has told you is a lie. The reason he and his angels left is because Abel would not let them turn the humans into slaves which was always his plan."

Matthew goes rigid. "I don't believe you." His voice is strained.

"Look at what they've turned you into. The Mattie I knew wouldn't want to kill these people that Cain has picked for his army against good."

Matthew's face twists. "Just stop!" He takes a couple steps back. Scotty tries to grab his arm to stop him from leaving but he shrugs him off. Matthew turns to run down the stairs. "You're wrong about Cain."

I watch Matthew leave with a heavy heart. Even after that I hope he can be saved.

"Is that the friend you mentioned earlier?" Michael's voice isn't mocking just simply curious.

"Yes." My voice is barely above a whisper and I haven't looked away from where Matthew was standing only moments ago.

"Well, good riddance. I should have stopped him from leaving. Now he's going to tell Cain to come faster or something." Scotty's bitter tone brings me back and I turn to face him.

"Matthew risked getting caught to tell us that Cain is coming and you're still going to say bad things about him?"

"Kathryn is right. The extra time that we gained thanks to Matthew gives us an advantage. I don't think capturing Matthew would have changed anything." Michael waits for Scotty to nod and then turns his attention to me. "Kathryn, what is the wild card that Matthew was talking about? Do you know any of their plans?"

"I remember that Matthew said Cain now had his wild card. I also remember Cain talking about a girl who would lead his army. Someone who has their memories and who is shy and quiet but observant, clever, and charismatic. Someone that everyone would follow without question. I just can't figure out who she is."

Scotty and Amanda stay very quiet and look at me. I look back and forth between their faces, uncomfortable under their stares. "What?"

They exchange a glance then Scotty steps forward. "Katie, that has to be you."

"No, it's not me." I at least know that much.

"How do you know that? Who else could it be?" Scotty approaches me cautiously as if I'm an injured dog that might attack at any moment.

"I just know it isn't me!" My head starts to hurt.

"There's no other girl with her memories that the angels have been watching other than Amanda and we both know it isn't her."

"And why not?" Amanda puts her hands on her hips.

"You're anything but shy and quiet."

"Fair point. I knew it had to be Katie anyway. Look at how we followed her lead at the gate and back at the mansion. She's a leader hiding as a follower."

An alpha wolf disguised as a lamb. I start to tremble.

Michael's eyes look very sad. "If the wild card has been dealt and Kathryn is the wild card then we could all be in a lot of danger right now."

"Katie isn't dangerous!" Scotty now glares at Michael.

"Maybe we should discuss this in private just in case. I'm sorry, Kathryn." Michael ushers Scotty and Amanda inside then turns to look at me apologetically.

I give him a half smile. He's right though. I can't be trusted. I am the wild card, the alpha wolf, the weapon. I could probably destroy everyone here. I don't even know what Cain did to me.

But I know who does.

I jump off the porch and set off in a sprint. I know Matthew will help me. I know he's not all bad. If I can convince him of that, maybe we can save each other.

Halfway through the forest my legs refuse to run anymore so I slow my pace. What am I going to do if Matthew can't or won't help me? What if I'm caught by Cain?

Lost in the swirls of my fears, I almost miss Matthew leaning against a tree off to my left. He picks at the bark on a twig in his hands and doesn't notice as I approach. "Mattie?"

If I startled him, he doesn't show it. He doesn't even look up as he speaks. "Go away, Katie. Go back to your friends while you can."

"I can't. You turned them against me, and I have questions which you have the answers to." I pull the stick from his hand so that he'll focus on me.

"There's nothing I can do to help you." He shoves passed me and begins walking in the direction of the mansion.

I follow and grab his arm. "I know that's a lie. You told me I had a surprise coming that I would like at first because I didn't know what it meant. I figured out that surprise was Scotty and Amanda coming to save me. You knew Cain wanted me to be with my friends and the other brainwashed people so he could use me to lead them back to him." Matthew stops and I stand in front of him where our chests are almost touching. My voice grows softer. "You knew his plan then, and you know his plans now. What makes me the wild card? How can he use me?"

Matthew looks into my eyes. I watch as he mentally tears in half, fighting with himself. I watch the struggle play across his face and hope that the side that will help me wins.

"Mattie, I know the real you is still in there. Don't fight me. We need each other We can be the winners here. I need you to help me."

"Katie, don't!" A sharp yell breaks the tense moment and Matthews internal battle ends without a determined outcome.

I turn to see Scotty and Amanda a couple yards behind me. "What are you doing here?"

"We could probably ask you the same thing." Amanda crosses her arms when she reaches me and glares at Matthew.

"You guys can't be here. You're going to get caught by Cain or I'm going to end up hurting you."

"Katie, I have carelessly lost you too many times. I don't care what you are, I'm not going to let you walk away again." Scotty reaches for my hand and Matthew recoils further into the cover of the trees.

The moment is interrupted by footsteps. Lots of footsteps. We all turn and face the mansion. A wave of white draws closer.

Cain's army of angels approach us. When they stop Cain steps out in front with a dark, twisted smile. His black attire a stain against the sea of white behind him. "Back so soon, Kathryn?"

My words get stuck in my throat. I hadn't had time to come up with a plan for if I happened to run into Cain. Now that it's happened, I freeze.

"Tell us what you did to her or I'll make you tell us." Amanda takes a few steps forward, fists clenched at her sides.

Cain ignores Amanda. "You know Kathryn, you might have been a great leader if you didn't let everyone manipulate you. I'm not talking about what we did, I mean how everyone around you who have no power use your emotions against you. Matthew was wrong when he chose you. You're too fragile. You are no longer useful to me so there's no reason for you to exist anymore." Cain comes closer, eyes locked on me. "Stay still." His words reach my ears at the same time I hear them in my mind.

Scotty and Amanda spring in front of me. "Don't you dare lay a hand on her or you won't have any hands." Amanda flicks open her pocketknife.

Cain focuses on Amanda. He looks her up and down then smiles almost amused. "You, however, have some guts. You wouldn't let people push you around, would you?" As I hear Cain's words my eyes grow wide as the realization hits me. "I'd much rather have you." Cain takes another step forward.

I throw myself in front of Amanda and find my voice. "No!"

"Of course, now you can speak." Cain looks annoyed.

Scotty rushes at Cain, but before he collides into him Matthew grabs him from behind and secures his arms into place. Cain approaches me until he is only a few feet away. "I suggest you move, Kathryn." He says through clenched teeth.

"No. You will not hurt my friend like you hurt me."

"You're not fooling anyone with this bravery act. Everyone here knows you are a coward. Now move!"

"I said, no!"

"Have it your way."

Step aside.

If I don't move, he is going to hurt me. I feel my left foot start to slide over, but as my body is about to shift out of the way a hand touches my shoulder.

I look up into green eyes. "Don't let him move you." Matthew puts himself between Cain and I. Scotty comes to my side and takes my hand. We all face Cain now.

The shock on his face looks out of place, almost comical if this wasn't such a serious situation. He quickly composes himself and anger alights in his reflective eyes. "What do you think you are doing, Matthew?"

"Choosing a side."

"You think any of them care about you? In their eyes you are the enemy. They'll turn on you without a second thought."

"What are the humans really for?"

"What does that matter?"

"Answer the question!" Anger radiates from Matthew. I want so badly to reach out and touch him, but he needs to hear this for himself.

"As our slaves, like what you are."

"I thought I was more important to you than just a disposable pawn." Matthew says, his voice thick with fury. "You promised me a place at your side and power."

"A place at my side as a favored pet. But right now, you're being a disobedient one. Get back here were you belong."

"This is where I belong. If you want them, you have to go through me." He reaches for my free hand. The muscles in his arms and back are tense.

Cain doesn't say anything. The moments of silence seem to stretch on to an impossible length. My unnecessary breaths stop, my chest tightens, and sweat beads up on the back of my neck.

Then Cain steps forward until he is almost chest to chest with Matthew who releases my hand. Cain stares down into Matthew's eyes and then he speaks in a low voice, "You asked for this."

Cain's hand shoots out and his fingers wrap around Matthew's throat. Instinctively Matthew clutches at Cain's hand but it's useless. Matthew begins to scream as light illuminates from Cain's hand. His eyes roll back into his head and his body begins to violently shake.

The light intensifies and it gets harder to see Matthew, but his screams continue to ring in my ears. Then in a flash the light is gone and so is Matthew.

No one speaks. I feel tears slip down my cheeks, but I can't move to wipe them away. I slowly bring myself to look at Cain who now stands in front of me with no one between us. He finally breaks the silence. "Move, Kathryn, or you're next."

CHAPTER THIRTY-TWO

My slack jawed expression hardens as I face Cain. I don't know what he did to Matthew, but I do know I will endure the same pain if it means protecting Amanda from him.

"I wonder, Kathryn, if you can scream as loud as he did, or if that small voice of yours only goes so high." Cain reaches for me, tucking two fingers under my chin. The same raised, irritated flesh that I saw on his neck covers his hand and snakes up his arm to disappear beneath his robe's sleeve. We lock eyes and I be sure to show him no fear. His hand lowers and I feel his long fingers slowly slide across my neck, squeezing just enough to hold me in place. Small prickles of pain start on the sensitive skin.

"Brother!" The seemingly time locked moment snaps as a new voice makes Cain look up past me.

"You're going to crash the party so soon, little brother?" Cain releases me and Scotty pulls me into his arms. I struggle to loosen his grip so I can see who is behind us.

More white robes. But my eyes pick out Michael standing up front with a fierce look in his eyes. Beside him is a man who looks like Cain only his brown hair is cut short and his stance isn't defensive but rather authoritative. This must be Abel.

An army of angels stand behind them. Three times as many as Cain has. Abel lifts his head and puts his shoulders back. "What you are doing here is wrong and it ends now."

"Ooh, you're so scary." Cain taunts but doesn't look amused at all. "How many people will you allow me to wipe from existence to stop me?"

Stand next to Cain.

I slip out of Scotty's arms and my feet start to walk toward Cain. What am I doing? Trying to be brave? I stand at his side and face my friends and Abel's army, all of whom are looking at me.

"Katie, what are you doing? You're going to get yourself killed!" Scotty starts to reach for me, but Amanda grabs his arm. He tries to break out of her grip but then she whispers something in his ear, and he stills.

I look at Michael and his eyes are filled with concern and confusion. He says something to Abel but doesn't take his eyes off me. Abel's eyes then meet mine, but only briefly before returning his attention back to Cain. "Let her go. No one else is going to get hurt because of your power-hungry greed."

"Well, you might want to stop me from doing this then." Cain's hand shoots up from his side and wraps around my throat. I pull at his hand as I feel the heat pulse from the grip. Scotty and Amanda rush forward but Samael and Jeremiah quickly restrain them. Dark spots cloud my vision, but the sea of white grows closer.

It gets harder to focus. Surrounding me are shouts from both sides but I can't make out any of the words. The pain and the heat intensify, and a scream tears its way out of me. The searing hot tears streaming down my face feel like they are burning through my skin.

I hang on the edge of blacking out and then all the pain stops, and I feel someone's arms supporting me. As my vision slowly returns Abel comes into focus. He looks down at me then walks away. I twist my head around and find Michael holding me. He brings me to my feet but keeps his hands around my waist. "Can you stand?"

"I... I think so." My breath is ragged, and I blush for appearing flustered. He lets go of me slowly and I test my legs by taking a few steps.

Then I remember the fight happening around me and I whirl around looking for Scotty. I spy him and Amanda standing back to back facing two groups of angels who have swords drawn. Are they Abel's or Cain's? I can't tell. Can anyone?

Something glowing orange in my peripherals begs for my attention. Before I can turn my head to face it, Michael swoops me around with his left arm and draws his sword with his right. His blade meets the fiery one of Jeremiah's with a clang and a hiss. I pull out of Michael's reach and stand behind him, shielded by his wings, as he places both hands on his sword. The metal alights with a crackle of lightening and blue tendrils twist around his hands on the hilt.

Get a sword.

I need to protect myself. I glance around at some of the fallen bodies of angels. Are they Cain's or Abel's? Are they dead? Can angels die? Violent flashes of blue and orange surround me as the battle climaxes. The ground shakes and knocks me off my feet. On my hands and knees I crawl to the closest body that still clutches a sword in its still hand. I take the blade, unfamiliar with the weight. I've only seen swords in movies before.

Attack Michael.

Now I know for sure something is wrong. I have no reason to attack the angel who's trying to save me. Even still

I rise to my feet and my arms lift the sword, ready to strike. I try to stop, I try to bring my arms down, but my willpower is useless.

Michael turns his head around to check on me. Jeremiah lays at his feet. When he sees my sword coming down at his face, he puts his up to block. The force of the metal meeting almost knocks me off my feet but all the strength in my body pushes against him.

"Kathryn, what are you doing?" he asks, glancing around for other threats.

"I don't know! I'm sorry! I can't stop myself!" I plead, willing him to believe me.

"Listen to me. Cain in controlling you, but you can stop this. Tell me what made you attack me?" Michael tries to keep his voice even.

I draw back my sword and swipe at him again, but he anticipates the move and blocks. "I don't know!" I begin to panic. I don't want to hurt him. Why can't I just stop?

"Yes, you do. Think. "My sword pushes closer and the blade sits at his neck. Our faces are only inches apart. He looks into my eyes, his face open. "They chose you because you're clever. Prove that to me."

I rack my brain. What's different? "The voice. There's a voice in my head. It's mine but not mine. Sometimes I can tell, but other times I can't." I grasp for words to make him understand.

"Okay, what did the voice tell you to do?"

"It told me to get a sword and then to attack you." My sword and I press closer.

"You did that. You got a sword and you attacked me. You did what it wanted so now you can stop."

"I can't! I tried!" The hysteria makes it hard to hold the sword still.

"Try again. Believe that you fulfilled the demand."

I do try. I believe with my whole existence that I did what Cain asked. I got the sword and I attacked Michael. I did it.

My muscles turn to liquid as the tension releases and I drop the sword to the ground. My body sways and Michael places a hand on my back to steady me. "See? You can beat him. You're strong."

"Where's Scotty?" I jerk my head around, swallowing the dizziness.

Before I find him a loud clap of thunder deafens my ears and everyone around me stills. Abel stands away from the fighting with Cain. As I study them together for the first time, it's almost unreal how similar they are without being twins. I suppose with them being the first humans born I shouldn't be surprised at the lack of gene variation.

"Enough!" Abel's voice rings out and everyone seems to freeze in time. All eyes turn to look at the two brothers to see what was going to happen. "I have pointed out to my brother Cain that he is outnumbered. Almost all his followers are down, and he has accepted defeat."

"Accepted isn't the word I would use. Just because you have won this time doesn't mean this is over." Cain takes a few steps away from his brother. Samael returns to his side and slowly a handful of other angels step away from what they were doing and flank Cain. I spy Amanda and Scotty who still have angels around them. They must be Abel's angels and they must have been protecting them.

"Just because I am not choosing to fight with you any longer does not mean you are going to go unpunished." Abel puts out his right hand and bright threads of light stream from his fingertips. "Cain, you and your followers will be cast into Hell and the Kingdom will be taken with us as we ascend into Heaven."

The light spreads from Abel and intertwines among Cain and the angels that stand with him. Their angry faces alight in the illumination. Cain stares out at me with steel eyes but allows the glow to consume him. In one violently bright flash, they're gone.

Abel focuses the power pouring out of his hand to the ground and it begins crackling beneath us. The movement causes me to wobble on my unsteady feet, but Scotty has made his way to me and catches me before I lose my balance.

"Things are finally being put right." His voice is strong, and I catch myself beaming. He's right. We fixed this.

The rumbling of the ground stops and Abel drops his hand to his side. All eyes look to him for reassurance that all is well. He glances around to all our faces then speaks in a captivating voice, "We have returned to Heaven. Everyone here who lost their memories because of Cain's plan will wake in the morning with them renewed. I will meet with them all to clear any confusion. All angels here can now return to their work."

The crowd of white dissipates slowly with soft murmurs of victory. The bodies from the battle have disappeared. Abel approaches our little group. "Michael, will you watch over Kathryn for a few moments? I would like to speak to Scott and Amanda privately."

Michael nods and I exchange an anxious look with Scotty. Amanda stares skeptically at everyone but then shrugs and follows Abel as he strolls toward Cain's mansion. My eyes don't leave them, and I watch as the distance grows between us. Scotty reluctantly let's go of me and jogs after them.

The silence hangs heavily in the air for a long stretch of time before I open my mouth. "Why are they talking about me?"

I can see Michael turn to face me out of the corner of my eye, but I don't look away from where my friends disappear into the dark house before me. "How do you know they are talking about you?" His tone is light and curious.

"Isn't it obvious since they left me behind?"

"Perhaps." He doesn't elaborate and I don't think asking will do any good.

After a few short moments his elbow nudges me and I finally face him. His left arm is extended for me to take. "Walk with me?"

I hesitate but then loop my arm in his. His arm is sturdy, but he's relaxed as he ushers me away from the mansion. "Where are we going?"

"For a walk in the meadow."

"Why?"

"To take your mind off things. Or maybe make it easier to talk about those things."

For a few moments I don't know what things he is talking about but then images of Matthew screaming in pain and disappearing flood my mind. I catch the sob that almost chokes its way up my throat. I also try to swallow the lump that is forming there so that I can get the words I need to ask out, but I can't.

Michael must know what I'm thinking because he doesn't wait for my question. "It's a strange gift Cain has. He is only supposed to use it on the people who are too evil even for Hell. It is the one thing that is worse than dying. Worse than living an eternity in Hell."

"What's worse than that?"

"Not existing. Cain can make it as if a person had never been born, never lived, never loved, never been loved, never meant anything to anyone. No one will ever remember them, and no one will ever know them. That is the worst thing that can happen to someone. To never be anything."

"But I haven't forgotten Mattie. I still know what he tried to do to save me."

"That's because you saw Cain do it with your own eyes. The memories will leave you more slowly."

"But I don't want to forget." The tears slip down my face

and I stop walking unable to make my feet move any further.

Michael let's my arm slide off his then comes to stand in front of me. He puts his hands lightly on my arms rubbing his thumbs in small circles. Nothing he can say could make this better so I'm thankful for his silent comfort.

I look up into Michael's eyes. Their silver depths hold me, and I can no longer take it. I fall forward wrapping my arms around Michael's waist and sob heavily. All the stress and heartache comes pouring out.

Michael tentatively puts his arms around me in return. He rests his head on top of mine and strokes my hair with his hands.

After a few minutes of this my tears run out, but I don't move. Michael is the one who breaks the moment. "Abel is almost finished with your friends."

I pull away and scrunch my eyebrows together. "How do you know?"

"He and I share psychic bond. We can send thoughts to each other when we need to."

"How?"

"That's just one of his gifts. He can do it with one angel, and he chose me."

"So, you only hear each other's thoughts when the other person lets you?"

"Exactly. It's sort of like instant messaging in your head." Michael extends his arm to me once again. I wipe my eyes on my sleeve then loop my arm through his.

We start walking back in the direction we came. Talking with Michael has really opened the flood gate to the hundreds of questions I didn't know I had. But now isn't the time. I have the rest of forever to get some answers.

As the mansion comes into view so does three figures. Abel, Scotty, and Amanda. Once Scotty sees me, he runs toward me. I break away from Michael and let Scotty's crashing embrace pick me up and spin me in a full circle.

As he sets me down his hands come up to cup my face. "I'm so happy that we're finally going to be okay again."

I smile and look up into his eyes. "Me too, Scotty."

"So now what?" Amanda's impatient voice makes me turn around and look at Michael again. He's looking at Abel who nods back at him.

Abel looks at Scotty and I then Amanda. "Michael and I need to talk about one more important question. If you three could kindly wait in the meadow, I would appreciate it."

"Why so many secrets?" Amanda stands in her iconic hands-on-hips position.

"I don't want to get your hopes up until something is decided. Just in case. Michael will come to speak with you when we are through. However, no matter the conclusion we reach I want to extend my deepest gratitude to you. You three are true blessings." Abel then turns to the mansion and Michael follows him without hesitation.

We stand still for a moment then Scotty takes my hand. "Let's go sit by the lake."

I start walking with him but then look over my shoulder to Amanda who hasn't moved yet. "Are you coming?"

"No offense, but I don't really want to be a third wheel to you lovebirds. I've got things to do, people to see, and all that."

I ponder that for a moment then shrug it off and turn to look ahead again.

CHAPTER THIRTY-THREE

Now that everything is finally right again, I allow myself to breathe and relax my tense body. Scotty and I sit on a dock at the lake in the center of the meadow. The sun is high in the sky instead of sinking low into the water, but I can't help myself from imagining we are back on Earth and it's our third anniversary where he took me on the perfect date before everything became complicated.

I touch the locket hanging from my neck. Scotty looks over at me. "You feel it too, don't you?" he asks.

"It feels peaceful right now like it did that day at the park."

"I know." He wraps his arm around me, and I lean into him thankful for the closeness. Even after everything this is where I want to be. I hope he knows that. After a comfortable silence Scotty's curious tone pulls me out of daydreams. "You never asked what we talked to Abel about."

He's right. I had wanted to, but I didn't think I could. "I didn't think you were allowed to tell me."

"You know I will always tell you anything. No secrets

among us, Katie."

"Okay, so what did you talk about? It was about me wasn't it?"

"Yeah it was. Abel is concerned about whose side you're on because you went to stand next to Cain at one point. I didn't understand why you did that either, but Amanda told me she thought you had some sort of plan. I don't know. It was weird."

"Does Abel think that I'm evil or something?" I sit up and look at Scotty scanning his face for any sign that I'm in trouble.

"Well I wouldn't say evil, but he wanted to be sure he could trust you. He believes that Cain had some sort of hold on you."

I think about my attack on Michael. Cain did have control, but I was able to fight back. Besides, that's all over now.

Scotty continues. "Abel also says that the control has been broken because no type of signal can transmit from Hell to Heaven." Scotty shrugs away my behavior which helps me relax again.

"I hate to break up the honeymoon guys, but that new angel wants to talk to us." I turn around to see Amanda watching us with her arms folded across her chest.

Scotty and I smile at each other and then stand up to follow her. "I wonder what he and Abel had to decide on." He ponders aloud as we make our hike back through the woods.

"Whether I'm trustable or not? Maybe they want to send me to Hell with Cain?" I shudder hoping that isn't the case.

"You told her about that?" Amanda punches Scotty in the arm playfully.

"Ow! Did you expect me not to?" He replies as he rubs his arm.

"I guess not. Seriously, Katie, there's nothing you need to

worry about. We already concluded you're safe."

The three of us finally reach the mansion and Michael is standing there all calm and perfect posture. His eyes track us until we're standing before him then he smiles. "You three are truly proof that miracles can be performed by everyday people." He walks forward and places a hand on each of our shoulders in turn. When his eyes meet mine, he lingers a second longer but then backs up to his original position.

"So, what happens now, angel man?" Amanda looks around skeptical of the tranquil setting.

"Well, from here you three can build your new lives. It's peaceful here and everyone is friendly. You can be whatever you want to be and have anything you want." Michael pauses as if pondering over his next words. "Or, just this once, Abel will allow me to bend the rules and you can go home to a time before your death and you can live what was meant to be your Earthly life." Michael only looks at Scotty and Amanda.

"Count me in! What do I do to board that train!" Amanda answers without hesitation then looks around anxiously awaiting the way out.

Michael hides a small smile. He waves his left hand to the side and a large mirror appears. "Stepping through this will take you home, but then the link will be broken, and you cannot return here until it is your time."

Amanda runs to the mirror. "Sorry guys, it's been fun here and all, but I have some unfinished business to attend to back on Earth. Of course, I guess you know that seeing as you're an angel and all." Amanda touches her hand to the reflective surface. I know she's anxious to go find Cassidy. It seems like it's been forever since I heard her tell that story to Scotty. She turns to face us. "You two coming?"

Scotty grabs my hand and takes a step forward. "Definitely." When I resist, he turns around to look at me. "Come on, Katie, we're going home."

"Scotty, I don't think I can go back."

"What? Katie, it's home. You can see your mom and dad and Marie again. We can be together again like before. No more Matthew or Cain or emotional controllers. Just us."

"I don't think I would be safe. Cain could get me on Earth like the first time." I look to Michael who nods in silent agreement.

"I can't let Kathryn return, only you and Amanda. Abel is concerned in keeping her protected and we can do that best here in Heaven.

Scotty's eyes fill with tears while mine flow freely down my face.

"Then I'll stay here with you." Scotty grasps my hand firmly in his.

I want that. More than anything. I've been fighting to keep Scotty and prove to him I love him despite what the angels led him to believe. All I'd have to do is ask him to stay and I know he would. I could control this situation in the way I want it.

But I'm learning that the power to control doesn't always mean getting your own way. I tried taking control of my life by killing myself and that hurt more people than I care to add up. I could take control of this and have Scotty stay, but if I let him return to Earth maybe he could fix some of the damage I caused. He could watch out for Cassie, take care of his mom, reassure my friends that they didn't cause my death.

But if I ask him to stay we wouldn't have to worry about those on Earth. We could be together...

The stronger side of me wins. "I can't ask you to do that. You need to go back to Earth and do what you were meant to do." As much as it hurts to say it, I know this is what's best.

"You want me to leave you...?" Misunderstanding crosses his face.

"It's not that I don't want you here with me, because I

231

know you would stay if I asked you to, but I don't want to hold you back from all that you want to do."

"That's not fair! What about all that you want to do?"

"I can play with my animals here, but your art is a big part of you, and I know you wouldn't be happy here without that competitive atmosphere that you have back on Earth. At least, not until you've fulfilled your dreams first. You've always wanted to make a name for yourself and I know you are capable of doing that."

"But that means nothing to me if I can't share it with you, Katie!"

"Scotty, I'm always going to be with you. I'm only a breath away. Anytime you need to talk, I'll always be right there to listen. And think about your mom. She's alone now. She needs you." The worst part is, I'm mostly pushing him away so he can achieve his dreams and reunite with his mom. Another small part of me still aches from the distance he put between us, even if it was emotion manipulation. The scars on our hearts are still there.

Scotty's shoulders slump because he knows I'm right. I know the thought of his mom alone hurts and I know he'd regret abandoning her later with this chance he has. "It's not going to be the same though."

"I know. But one day it will be again."

"You think so?"

"I know so. I can wait for you to return as an old man." I allow a small playful smile to play across my lips.

Scotty grabs me and hugs me tightly to him. "I love you, Katie."

"I love you too."

"Okay, this is getting to mushy for me." Amanda makes a face. "I'll see you guys later." She sticks her hand through the reflection then steps through and disappears.

Scotty turns from where she disappears to face me again.

"So, this is really what you want?" He looks at me level and analyzes my face for any signs of uncertainty.

I take a deep breath and let it out, composing myself. I look him in the eyes and smile. "Yes." And I mean it. I know this is hard for him, but I can feel the relief from him that he didn't have to make the decision alone. I know he'll be happy with this second chance at life.

He sighs but smiles back. "I'll miss you."

"I'll miss you too."

"Promise you'll wait for me?"

"Of course, pinky promise." I pause a moment. "But try to find Amanda when you're not too busy attending art shows. She needs someone to keep her out of trouble. I'd be okay if that was you."

His smile widens and he hugs me one last time. He let's go and touches his hand to my cheek. I lean into it and close my eyes just for a moment. His lips touch mine so softly and in my head I think about changing my mind and asking him to stay, but I know I wouldn't forgive myself for stopping him from pursuing this life he wants and deserves.

He pulls away and I open my eyes to see his crystal blue ones looking back into mine. Then he turns to the mirror. He walks slowly to it, but he doesn't look back at me. I'm glad he doesn't because I don't want him to see me crying again.

The mirror shimmers as I watch Scotty walk through without hesitation. I know I made the right choice by letting him go, but I'm going to miss him.

The mirror fades and I feel Michael's presence beside me. "I assume you know how everyone's life is going to go, and that you probably can't tell me details, but does he do okay back on Earth?" I ask without taking my eyes off where the mirror used to be.

"He lives a good life." When he doesn't elaborate, I start to wonder if that's all he's going to say. I finally look up at

Michael and he is looking back at me. "That was a very selfless thing you did, Kathryn. You will see him again one day." Michael reaches over and wipes away a tear sliding down my cheek. We stand in silence for a few moments. "Would you like me to walk you home?"

"Not yet. I need a few minutes here alone."

"As you wish. I'll be around if you need me."

"Thank you, Michael." He nods and turns to walk away. I look back at the empty space in front of me and let the last of my tears slip silently down my face.

Smile.

I look up into the warm sunshine and let the smile slowly spread across my face.

Epilogue – Scott

I open my eyes and things begin to come into focus. I'm standing outside with a large group of people. In front of me is a hole dug into the soft black dirt of the cemetery. Katie's casket sits beside it.

Her mom stands beside me, trembling with grief. I reach out and grip her shoulder in comfort, noticing the gold bangle still dangling around my wrist. She places her shaking hand on mine then looks up at me. "I've never noticed how beautiful your silver eyes are before."

Shock makes me drop my hand. I inch away from the crowd of people and study the bracelet. The spike is still embedded into my skin. Panic rises in my chest but then sinks. This bracelet is used to travel from Earth to the Kingdom.

I look up at the gloomy overcast skies. A few drops of rain land on my face. "There's no need to cry now, Katie." A small hole breaks through in the clouds and a sliver of sunlight streams down onto the gathered friends and family.

"That's better."

Coming soon…

You've witnessed the battle, but can you survive the war?

Keep an eye out for The Other Angels Book Two!

Acknowledgments

Firstly, I want to thank you, the reader, for choosing my book to read. Your support in my writing dreams means the world. If you could do me one more favor and leave a review, I would be most grateful!

I also want to thank my tech support boyfriend, Anthony. Without him, I wouldn't have a website, blog, formatted book, social media promo pictures and videos, the list goes on. I'd be lost. So, thank you, and I love you.

I want to thank my beta readers for their early insight.

Thank you to my editor and book trailer designer, Michele Sagan. Your amazing quality of help has brought this book to the next level.

Thank you to my cover designer, Ryan Rinsler. I immediately fell in love with the design you created. Thank you for putting up with my endless questions and comments.

Thank you to the Writing Community of Twitter. You all make me feel welcomed and supported every day.

Lastly, thank you to all of you who believed in this book even when I didn't. Your push and encouragement is what completed this project. I couldn't have made it this far without all of you. So, thank you.

About the Author

Ashley Nicole resides in a small town in West Virginia with her boyfriend and spoiled kitten, River. By day, she works at her local vet clinic and by night she pours her imagination out onto a page. She has dreamed of becoming a published author for so long and with this debut, she has finally made it a reality. She has plans for dozens of other stories ranging from fantasy to dystopian to thriller and she hopes you'll come along for the ride!

You can keep updated on new books and writing tips by visiting www.ashleynicolewrites.com. Connect with her on her social medias Twitter, Facebook, Instagram, and Pinterest.

As a writer, Ashley's goal is to share everything she learns on her author journey. She posts regular writing tip articles on her Medium profile.

www.ingramcontent.com/pod-product-compliance
Lightning Source LLC
Chambersburg PA
CBHW061613100726
47898CB00002B/640